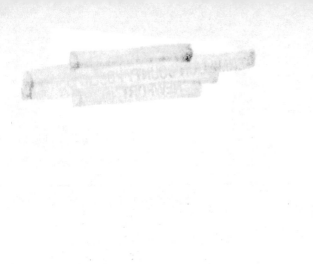

Tiles
and
Tribulations

TAMAR MYERS

Tiles and Tribulations

A DEN OF ANTIQUITY MYSTERY

AVON BOOKS

An Imprint of HarperCollinsPublishers

AVON BOOKS
An Imprint of HarperCollins*Publishers*
10 East 53rd Street
New York, New York 10022-5299

ISBN: 0-7394-3352-0

Printed in the U.S.A. 84995

For my three loving children.
It couldn't have been easy
having me for your mama.

Sarah
David
Dafna

Acknowledgments

My limited knowledge of Portuguese tiles was acquired during a trip to Portugal. I was privileged to visit many castles and palaces, as well as the fabulous National Museum of Azulejo in Lisbon.

I would like to thank members of the Charleston Authors Society for their support and encouragement, particularly Mary Alice Monroe and Nina Bruhns.

Tiles and Tribulations

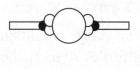

1

My best friend., C.J., is deathly afraid of Apparition Americans. Unfortunately, her not-so-new house on Rutledge Avenue has at least one very vocal semitransparent resident. I told C.J. to expect spirit lingerers when buying a two-hundred-year-old Charleston mansion, but no, the big gal wouldn't listen.

Since I had warned her, I didn't feel it was my responsibility to attend the silly séance she had planned. It's not that I don't believe in Apparition Americans—I do. My own house is haunted, in fact. But mine is a benign presence who contents himself with jangling a bunch of keys and pacing up and down my long, narrow upstairs hallway. C.J.'s unwelcome tenant, on the other hand, wails like the banshee she might well be, and once she even touched C.J. with hands as cold as Popsicles.

So intimidating is C.J.'s spirit, that my friend has had a devil of a time getting a contractor to do some necessary remodeling. Three burly men have quit in the time it takes to change a light bulb, much less re-vamp a nineteen forties style kitchen. But the really strange thing is that, since the last workman ran off the job—leaving his tool belt behind—the ghost has taken on the remodeling job herself. I know this sounds bizarre, but C.J. swears it's true. She claims she comes home from work and finds wallboard re-placed, paint scraped, tiles caulked, you name it. So far the repairs are remarkably like the ones C.J. wanted the contractor to do, although this has done nothing to ameliorate C.J.'s terror.

At any rate, my objection to the séance had to do with the fact that it was to be conducted, not by some proven expert in the field of the paranormal, but by Madame Woo-Woo. She was a self-styled psychic whose name C.J. had gotten from my mother, who found it advertised in the Yellow Pages. Madame Woo-Woo's ad claimed she was *the* expert in con-vincing confused Apparition Americans that their jobs on the earth were over, and it was time for them to return to the spirit realm. Madame Woo-Woo claimed a ninety-nine point nine percent success rate, and even offered a money back guarantee. At the prices she charged, she should have given her cus-tomers gold plaques certifying that their houses were hant-free, as politically incorrect locals might say.

I wouldn't even have been a part of the Madame Woo-Woo brouhaha, were it not for the fact that the medium had demanded that there be nine warm bodies at the séance, besides her own. She claimed it had something to do with numerology, but frankly, I suspected the woman was after more clients. Besides, it was the last night of *Survivor IV*, and I just had to see who won the million dollars. Yes, I know, I could have taped it, but it just isn't the same thing. Ask any sports enthusiast.

You can imagine my irritation then, when my mother called me at work to put the screws to me.

"Mama," I said, trying to keep in mind the thirty-six hours of agonizing labor she endured to produce me, "I am *not* going to the séance, and that's final."

"Are you afraid, Abby? Is that the problem, dear?"

"Of course I'm not afraid!"

"Abby, darling," Mama said, pouring on the sugar, "C.J. is your best friend. She needs you."

"Mama, the Woo-Woo woman says there has to be nine of us, besides her. Whether or not I show up is a moot point."

"What was that, dear? Did you say something about mooing?"

"Moot," I said as mutely as I could. I own The Den of Antiquity, a thriving antique business on King Street, in Charleston, South Carolina. The aforementioned C.J., besides being my best friend, is my employee. At the moment she was standing just a few yards away, closing a sale on an eighteenth-century highboy.

"Well, it might not be such a moot point after all,

Abby, because I've found six others, besides you and I and C.J. We're good to go."

"What six others?"

"Well for one, there is the real estate agent who sold C.J. the house. Since he didn't warn her about the ghost, he has a responsibility to be there, don't you think?"

"I'll buy that. Who are the remaining five?"

"The Heavenly Hustlers."

"What the hell is the Heavenly Hustlers?" I braced myself for Mama's answer. Last year she ran off to be a nun—they wouldn't accept her—*and* dated a gigolo named Stan. With her track record, I wouldn't be at all surprised if the Heavenly Hustlers turned out to be proselytizing prostitutes.

"Oh, Abby, don't you ever listen to a word I say?"

"Occasionally. But I don't remember anything about Heavenly Hustlers. Mama, you haven't gotten yourself tangled up with some kind of cult, have you?"

"The Hustlers," Mama huffed, "are a group of retired folk, like myself, who aren't content to sit on their duffs all day and twiddle their thumbs. Or do nothing but watch TV. We go to lectures, art exhibits, you name it. Last month we took a basket-weaving class from one of the Gullah women who sells those sweetgrass baskets at The Market. Next week we're driving up together to Brookgreen Gardens, near Myrtle Beach, to see the sculpture collection. In the meantime, we'd be glad to help C.J. out with her séance. Of course we can't all make it on such short notice—there are twelve in our group altogether—but the six of us can."

I sighed, both with relief and resignation. It was a relief that Mama had found a group of like-minded folks to hang out with, but attending C.J.'s séance was going to be a major bummer. I would program the VCR to tape *Survivor IV*, but if my husband Greg did anything to screw that up—like substitute a sports video—there would be yet another Apparition American for Madame Woo-Woo to exorcise.

Don't get me wrong; I absolutely adore my new husband, Greg Washburn. A former police detective up in Charlotte, North Carolina, he is now a shrimp boat captain in Mt. Pleasant, South Carolina, just outside of Charleston. Greg is both my lover and my best friend, and I am very lucky to have him in my life.

I know just how fortunate I am, because for over twenty years I was married to Buford Timberlake, who was more timber snake than man. That marriage produced two wonderful, but trouble-producing children, who are now both away at college. At any rate, Buford would never have put up with my mother living with us.

"Okay, Mama, I'll be there. What time is it again?"

"Eight, dear. But I was planning for us to get there a few minutes early and help C.J. put together some snacks. Maybe a nice dessert."

"I'm sure your Heavenly Hustlers would appreciate that."

"Oh, it's not for them, dear—although they're welcome to eat some too. It's for Madame Woo-Woo. C.J. says she's very temperamental."

I smiled to myself. C.J. isn't particularly temperamental herself, but she is a radish or two short of a relish tray.

"Yeah, well, getting there early is probably a good idea in any case. I want to check under the table to make sure Madame Woo-Woo hasn't wired it."

There was a pause, which meant Mama was thinking—always a dangerous situation. A wise Abby would have gotten off the line while the getting was good. Alack, I was too well-mannered to hang up on Mama.

"What will you be wearing tonight?" she finally asked.

"Clothes." Good manners did not preclude sarcasm.

Mama sighed dramatically. "I'm sure what you have on is fine, dear."

I wrinkled my nose at the phone receiver. I will always be inappropriately dressed to Mama. She is caught in a nineteen fifties time warp and wears cinch-waist dresses with full-circle skirts puffed up by yards of starched crinolines. Standing at five feet even, sans patent leather pumps, she looks like a miniature, and very well-preserved, version of June Cleaver. Mama even wears a single strand of pearls, a gift my father gave her the year he died. That the beads outlasted even my first marriage is a wonder, given the fact that Mama never takes them off—not even to shower.

"I'm wearing jeans," I said. "If Madame Woo-Woo doesn't like it, she can lump it."

"It wasn't the psychic I was thinking about," Mama said. "It's C.J.'s ghost."

"What? Apparition Americans are into fashion?"

"C.J. has seen the ghost twice, Abby, and both times she was wearing antebellum clothes. So that's how the Heavenly Hustlers and I will be dressing. We want to make C.J.'s ghost feel comfortable."

"And C.J.?" I said the girl's name a mite too loud and she glanced my way.

"She's wearing a hoop skirt as well."

"Mama, where did y'all get clothes like that on such short notice?"

"From Ella Nolte. She's one of the Hustlers. She's also a mystery writer and has connections with the theater department at the College of Charleston."

"Ella Nolte? I've never heard of her."

"That's because you don't read mysteries, dear."

"I don't read fiction altogether, Mama. I mean, what's the point? It's all made up." I was only pulling her leg, and Mama knew it.

"So how about it, Abby, are you game?"

"I'm game," I growled. Then I gasped. My worst nightmare had just walked through the door of my shop.

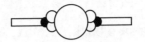

2

"Abby, what is it?"

"It's Buford!"

"Buford who?"

"*The* Buford, Mama. My ex."

"Hide!" Mama hung up her phone.

I glanced around my shop. There are plenty of places to hide in an antique store, especially given my size. I am four feet, nine inches in my stocking feet, and tip the scale at one hundred pounds the day after New Year's. I could easily fit into an armoire, even a dresser drawer.

Then it hit me. Buford lived all the way up in Charlotte. His presence down here in Charleston could mean only one thing.

"What happened!" I cried. I was on Buford like white on rice. He didn't even see me coming.

"Abby!"

"Is it Charlie? Is it Susan? Oh my God, there's been an accident, hasn't there? How bad is it?"

Buford took a step back. "Relax, Abby, it's not the kids."

"Then what *is* it?" I admit to living in perpetual fear that one, or both, of my two children will be involved in a horrible car wreck. As I've told them both a million times, it isn't their driving that worries me, but "others." By that I mean other teenagers and young adults—ones whose overly protective mothers didn't insist that they take drivers' training. Then of course, there are those folks, of any age, who indulge in road rage.

Buford regarded me under hooded lids. His had once been a handsome face, which in recent years had become fleshy.

"I'm on vacation, Abby."

"Right. And I'm Julia Roberts. Pleased to meet you."

Who was he trying to kid? Buford wouldn't know what vacation was if it sneaked up behind him and bit him on the butt. The man never quit moving; before he packed on the extra weight, he used to put his socks on while walking.

Our honeymoon was a three-day cruise to the Bahamas and Buford jumped ship at the end of the first day, so he could get back to work. And just in case you're wondering, *that* was quick was well. I didn't even warrant a "wham, bam, thank you, ma'am." Just a wham.

Buford smiled, his jowls retreating slowly. "I really am on vacation, Abby. After Tweetie died," he said, referring to his second wife, "I decided to take some time off and smell the roses."

"Uh-huh."

"I know you don't believe me, but it's true. The kids—particularly Susan—kind of pushed this trip on me. By the way, I saw both kids this morning, and they're doing fine."

So that was it! With their stepmother out of the picture, the kids figured they could maneuver their daddy and I into a reconciliation. I could understand their desire—even with Buford as one of the players—but it wasn't going to happen. Dr. Laura and John Ashcroft would dance naked together in Times Square before I hitched up with the timber snake. Heck, I'd hitch up with Laura or John before I got back together with Buford.

"It isn't going to happen," I said calmly.

"What's that?"

"The kids' ploy. I'm not falling for it."

He frowned for a moment, then his florid face shone with enlightenment. "Ah, so that's what you're thinking. No offense, Abby, but I'm not interested in a relationship either."

"You're not?"

"You sound disappointed, Abby."

"I am most certainly *not* disappointed! I'm merely surprised." While I was telling the truth, I must admit that one can be flattered even by unwanted attention.

"Well, here I am. I've got four days at my disposal. Do you have any recommendations—as regards sightseeing, I mean."

"The Charleston Visitor's Center is at 375 Meeting Street. They can tell you a lot more than I can."

A divorce lawyer by profession, Buford is not easily dismissed. "I was planning to make them my next stop. I just thought you might have some personal favorites. In particular, I was wondering about restaurants. I was hoping we could do lunch. My treat, of course."

Charleston is, without a doubt, the most charming city in the country. The beauty of its architecture and gardens is famous worldwide. Since the majority of her visitors have discerning tastes, it is no surprise that the city is home to some of the finest restaurants in North America.

"Do I get to choose the restaurant?"

Buford chuckled. "Absolutely."

"How about lunch tomorrow, one o'clock, Magnolias?" I was already planning my selections. For the first time I was going to have no compunctions about ordering anything I wanted on the menu. Maybe even everything. After all, when Buford dumped me in favor of Tweetie—a woman half my age and ninety percent silicone—he left me in a financial bind.

Actually, that's an understatement. Buford was not just plugged into the good old boy system, he had more connections than a box of Tinker Toys. He ended up with the house, the cars, custody of our seventeen-year-old son, and even the family dog. All I got to keep were my clothes—only because they didn't fit Tweetie—and three thousand dollars I'd managed to squirrel away into a personal account.

"Sounds good," Buford said.

Just wait until he saw the bill.

C.J. waltzed over to me the second the shop door closed on Buford's expanding bottom. "Ooh, Abby, I'm so proud of you!"

I smiled nonchalantly. "Thanks. I'm pretty proud of myself. The old Abby would have picked up that Civil War sword over there, and stuck it where the sun doesn't shine. Or better yet—"

"No, Abby. I meant I'm proud of you for agreeing to come to my séance tonight. I know how afraid you are of ghosts."

"*Me*? You're the one who—hey, wait a minute, how did you know I agreed to come?"

"I heard you talking to your mama. Besides, Madame Woo-Woo told me you'd resist coming at first, but that you'd finally give in."

"She did?"

"Well, she didn't say *you*—not exactly, at any rate. But she did say there would be skeptics whose minds would be changed."

"Frankly, dear, that sounds a little vague to me. I read somewhere that psychics and fortunetellers are

often very skilled at giving answers that can be inter-
preted a variety of ways. The article also said they
tend to ask leading questions. In other words, they've
got great powers of observation, and good people
skills, but they're not privy to any more information
than the rest of us."

"Ooh, Abby, Madame Woo-Woo knows everything."

Business seemed to have dropped off momentarily,
so I decided to take advantage of the lull and treat my
young assistant to the benefits of my experience. Like
I said, she's smart as a whip, but she doesn't cook
with all four burners.

"C.J., dear, just how well did you research this
Madame Woo-Woo? Did you check her references?"

She looked like a sheep that had been given the
task of cloning a human. She scratched her head, and
then looked at the door, as if longing for customers to
walk through.

"Well?" I demanded. "Did you at least ask to speak
to someone—anyone—who's hosted a séance for her
before?"

C.J. hung her head. "No," she said in a tiny voice.

"And what about this group—the Heavenly Hustlers—that Mama rounded up. What do you know
about them?"

"I love your Mama, Abby. Any friends of hers are
friends of mine."

"That's very generous of you," I said, feeling the
need to ease up. "But let's just both be careful, shall

we? Mama has a tendency to hook up with some real characters. And as for Madame Woo-Woo, neither of us wants to be a seer's sucker, now do we?" I laughed pleasantly at my little joke.

C.J. shook her head vigorously. "Cousin Alvin's fiancée up in Shelby invented seersucker, and it hurt something awful."

I raised my right eyebrow. C.J.'s litany of Shelby stories is what sets her apart from the rest of the population. Normally we try to discourage these tall tales, but I'd always wondered who invented seersucker. And why.

"Please," I said. "Tell me all."

"Well, she was wearing a dress made out of regular material, you see. Something smooth like silk or nylon, but I forget which. Anyway, she was running late to church one Sunday and she noticed that her dress had a wrinkle in the skirt. So Brenda—that's Alvin's fiancee's name—took the steam iron and started ironing out the wrinkle. Only she didn't take the dress off first, see? And she had a whole lot of cellulite—" C.J. hung her head so low her chin rested against her chest. "Abby, I just made that up—about Cousin Alvin's wife inventing seersucker, I mean. But she really does have a lot of cellulite."

"So you don't know who invented seersucker?"

"I'm afraid not, Abby. But according to *Webster's* the word seersucker has been part of the English language since 1722. It comes originally from the Persian phrase *shir-o-shakar*, and literally means 'milk and sugar.' "

It didn't surprise me that my friend would know the dictionary definition of the word. After all, she'd memorized the book her senior year in high school, in preparation for college. The collegiate version, of course. It did surprise me, however, that C.J. backed out of one of her Shelby stories. That just wasn't like her. Only last month she'd sworn on a stack of bibliographies (C.J. is not all that religious) that her Granny Ledbetter and Queen Victoria were bosom buddies, and that it was at one of the palace teas that Granny Ledbetter invented cottage cheese.

"C.J., dear, is something wrong? Just a minute ago you came bounding over to me like a gazelle on speed, and now you seem to have lost your spunk."

"Abby, you remember how that voodoo priestess in Savannah said I had the second sight?"

"Diamond? C.J., she wasn't exactly a voodoo priestess. She was a retired schoolteacher who liked to entertain tourists."

"But she said I had the second sight, Abby, and you know I do."

"Then why the need to hire a psychic?" I asked gently.

"Ooh, Abby, you can be so silly sometimes. Just because I have the second sight doesn't mean I can talk to ghosts."

"You're quite right. But you still haven't answered my question. What's wrong?"

"I was getting to that, Abby. My second sight tells me that something horrible is going to happen at my house tonight."

The shiver that ran up my spine didn't stop there. It made it all the way up to my scalp where it danced a rousing polka.

"So why not cancel, C.J.?"

The big gal did her best to disguise her feelings, but there was no mistaking the pity in her eyes. "Because it's destiny, Abby. There's nothing I can do to stop what's going to happen."

"We'll just see about that," I said.

3

Ella Nolte might be a famous mystery writer, but she was unable to get the costumes she promised from the College of Charleston. Fortunately another of the Hustlers, a doctor with a mouthful of a name, came to the rescue. Dr. Francis Lloyd Whipperspoonbill belongs to the War of Northern Aggression Reenactment Brigade. Reenactment groups are common in the South—and I'm told in the North as well—but WNARB, as this group calls itself, goes one step further. Its members not only reenact famous Civil War battles, but they rehearse possible future battles—which smacks a bit of treason, if you ask me.

At any rate, Dr. Whipperspoonbill was able to provide authentic Civil War uniforms for the men and period dresses for we ladies. WNARB prides itself on authenticity, and the women who attend the reenactments stand along the sides of the battlefield, often crying real tears. Southern women don't sweat, we merely dew, but the WNARB women produce enough dew to drown all of Dixie. The dresses Mama and I were loaned smelled of mothballs and dried dew.

It is virtually impossible to drive with a hoop skirt jutting up in front of one's face, so Mama and I walked the eight long blocks from my house to C.J.'s. Fortunately, a skirt designed to hide ankles can hide shoes as well. I wore my inflatable-sole Nikes. Mama, who is more set in her ways than a Hollywood handprint, wore a pair of pink pumps. You can bet that underneath her hoops she wore her precious crinolines.

Mama carried a cake, and I carried a tray of biscuits and ham. You wouldn't believe the looks we got. The occupants of automobiles either honked or gave us the thumbs up, and pedestrians, mostly tourists, smiled and invariably had something to say. A few asked if we were selling refreshments, but the majority were just eager to sign up with our tour company. Mama, ever willing to make a buck, especially through eccentric means, told everyone to meet her at The Market promptly at nine the next morning and she would lead them on a tour they would never forget.

It was a typical summer evening in Charleston, and we arrived at C.J.'s tired and drenched in dew. At one point, in an effort to dab at my forehead with a hanky, I dragged my sleeve across the cake. The message, which had originally read "Goodbye Ghost," now read "Goodbye host."

Tired as we were, Mama and I both recoiled when C.J. flung open the door of her dilapidated Georgian-style mansion.

"How come you're not in costume?" I demanded.

C.J. stepped aside to let us enter. It was only marginally cooler inside. One of the many things C.J. needed to do while restoring the house was to add central air. Granted, there was no air-conditioning in the eighteenth century, but folks were always fainting. Seems to me that should have been a clue.

"None of the dresses fit," C.J. said, taking the goodies from us. "Back then most women were y'all's size, not mine."

I had my shoes inflated to the max, so Mama was still only three inches taller. Nonetheless, she took umbrage at being lumped with me.

"I am not Abigail's height," she said squaring her shoulders and puffing her chest. It was then that I noticed Mama was still wearing her pearls.

C.J. shrugged. "The men couldn't fit in their costumes either, except for Dr. Whippersnapper."

"That's Whipperspoonbill," Mama said, and patted her pearls in agitation.

"Whatever," I said. "C.J., in which room is the séance being held?"

"Madame Woo-Woo asked that it be held around a table, so I thought we'd use the formal dining room."

"Are we the first to arrive?"

"Yes, silly, the séance doesn't start for another half an hour."

"Have any of the Heavenly Heifers been here before?"

"That's Heavenly Hustlers," Mama hissed.

C.J. shook her massive head. "No, Abby. The Heavenly Hosts have never been here."

"How about Madame Woo-Woo?"

C.J. nodded. "She came by yesterday to look around. Mozella let her in."

Mama flushed. "Actually, dear, I loaned my key to a friend and had her let Madame Woo-Woo in. You don't mind dear, do you?"

"Of course not, Mozella. You know I trust your judgment."

Too bad I didn't. "C.J." I said, "didn't it ever occur to you that she might be rigging the place?"

"Ooh, Abby, you're always so skeptical."

"I second that," Mama said. She handed C.J. the cake.

C.J. took the cake, but her eyes widened as she noticed the ominous message for the first time. "Oh, my God, I knew it! I told you, didn't I, Mozella?"

Mama turned to me so that I could see her roll her eyes, but she addressed C.J. "The cake doesn't mean anything, dear—except that my daughter's a bit on the clumsy side."

"Thanks, Mama," I said, and handed her the tray of

biscuits and ham. Then, leaving her to reassure C.J., I wandered off on a reconnaissance mission.

It didn't take me more than a couple of minutes for me to make my discovery. Taped to the underside of the dining room table was a small cassette player.

"Oh, ladies," I called. "I found it! I found Madame Woo-Woo's ju-ju."

C.J. and Mama set the food down and trotted over. C.J. crawled under the table to join me, but Mama had yet to learn that the trick to managing the hoops in this case was to sit and let the hoops collapse around her. Instead, Mama was barely able to stick her head under the table, while the hoops ballooned behind her like the spread tail of a tom turkey.

"What is it, Abby? I can't see. What does a ju-ju look like?"

"Ju-ju just means a spell, Mama. Magic. In this case, it's a mini tape recorder."

"Ooh, play it Abby," C.J. urged.

I pushed the play button. For a second or two nothing seemed to happen. Then gradually, I heard what sounded like faint wind. After about a minute the wind became louder to the point that it sounded like a level four hurricane. Then suddenly it stopped, just as a female voice began to speak.

"I am Sarah MacGregor," it said in a bad Scottish accent. "I am mistress of this house. What, pray tell, are you doing here?"

There followed a long pause.

"But I did not invite you here. I am afraid I must insist that you leave," Sarah MacGregor said, her voice more sad than strident.

Another interminable silence.

"But that cannot be. Surely you are mistaken!"

I could have taken a power nap during the next pause.

"Very well then," the taped voice finally said, "have it your way. But be forewarned, there will be consequences—some of which may be quite dire. I am not responsible for these consequences."

I fast-forwarded through the next silent stretch. I did a darn good job of guessing, and only had to rewind for two words.

"This is *my* house," Sarah MacGregor said in her thick, but uneven, burr. "I will not leave. It is you who must do so."

I misjudged the length of the next pause, but that was soon rectified.

"What sort of gift?" Sarah asked.

The response she received was brief.

"Yes, a gift of money would be very nice. The repairs on this home are outrageous."

"Ooh," C.J. cooed, "Madame Woo-Woo's ju-ju is going to get me some moolah."

I smiled. "I don't think so, dear. We haven't heard the end of the tape."

"Play it!" Mama ordered. She was having a hard time maintaining her stoop.

I pushed the button again.

"Aye," Sarah MacGregor said right on cue, "there is one among ye that seems to be more sensitive than most—"

"You see, Abby?" C.J. cried. "That would be me! I'm the one with the second sight."

"With no sense," Mama muttered.

I had to rewind a bit.

"—more sensitive than most. Her name—I can see it in my mind—is Wo-wo. No! It's more like Woo-Woo. Yes, that is it! Madame Woo-Woo! She is the one to whom the gifts must be entrusted."

A brief pause ensued.

"Large gifts, I'm afraid," Sarah MacGregor said, her voice taking on an ominous tone. "Or the curse of the MacGregors will be upon ye."

There was another brief pause, followed by the sound of more wind. I pushed the off button.

"C.J., you wouldn't happen to have a cassette recorder of your own, would you?"

"I do, Abby. And I have oodles of cassettes too. Do you like Barry Manilow?"

I refused to answer her question on the grounds it might incriminate me. "Any blank cassettes?"

"Of course. What is it, Abby? What do you have planned up those smelly sleeves of yours?"

I glanced at my watch in the dim light beneath the table. There was still a good twenty minutes before the first of the Heavenly Herd was due to arrive.

"Just wait and see," I said.

The first to arrive was the infamous Ella Nolte. I was under the table putting the final touches on my handiwork when the doorbell rang, but I managed to scoot out and plump my hoops in the nick of time.

I caught my breath when I saw Ms. Nolte. She was middle-aged, tall, with frizzy blond hair, and I knew her from somewhere—ah yes, the jacket photo of her latest book. Authors' names don't stay with me long, but their books do, especially if they are particularly bad. This author's latest was a total waste of pulp, and I'd literally thrown the book across the room. The woman's style is far too frivolous for my tastes. Who needs a bunch of puns, when a plain old plot will do just fine? And her protagonist—the overbearing owner of a bed and breakfast, somewhere in Indiana, I believe—has a tongue that could slice cheese.

Mama introduced us with a good deal of enthusiasm. Apparently she was a big fan of Ms. Nolte's books, a fact that surprised me. The only reading material I've seen in Mama's house is the Holy Bible, and a rack of well-thumbed *Reader's Digest* magazines in the bathroom.

"This is my daughter Abigail Washburn," she said,

and not without a little pride, I am pleased to note. "Her last name used to be Timberlake, and she's sort of famous too. She owns two antique stores. They're both called The Den of Antiquity, but one is up in Charlotte, and the other is down here."

Ms. Nolte had a long nose—longer than the main runway at Charleston International—and she looked down its length with beady eyes of nondescript color. Then she snorted.

"Interesting dresses. They look almost real."

"They are," Mama said. "Francis supplied them."

"Harrumph!" She didn't just clear her throat; she actually said the word. "Just because Dr. Francis Lloyd Whipperspoonbill supplied them—well, you know what I mean."

"Not really," said Mama.

"I certainly don't," I said.

Ms. Nolte's beady eyes bored into mine. "I was at one of his Civil War reenactments once, out at Charles Towne Landing. I was in the restroom when some of the ladies in supposedly period costume came in and started chatting among themselves. Guess what I learned?"

"What?" Mama and I cried in unison.

"They had pouches sewn into their skirts in which they kept ice bags. You know the reusable kind you stick in the freezer and then use in picnic chests."

"What a clever idea," Mama said. Neither of us was about to divulge that we had food storage bags

pinned to the undersides of our skirts. Our bags, however, contained ordinary ice cubes.

"*And* those dresses had zippers."

"Well, ours don't have zippers," I said.

If the boring eyes were searching for oil, they were
out of luck. "I know who you are. I was in your shop
once. You have the flaky assistant, right?"

C.J. was standing right there, for crying out loud. I
wanted to reach up and slap Ms. Nolte until her curls
went straight.

"*This* is my assistant," I said, pushing C.J. forward
for her introduction. "Her name is Jane Cox. And this
is her house."

The famous writer sniffed. "Then it must be a different shop I was thinking of. This one had a lot of—
well, junk."

"Are you sure?" I asked through clenched teeth.
"About the junk, I mean."

Ella Nolte's gaze made that long trip down her
snout again. "I know a little something about antiques. The shop I'm thinking of sold junk."

Mama had the grace to whisk the wicked Hustler
from the room. Meanwhile I debated whether or not I
should say anything to C.J., or leave well enough
alone. C.J. settled the matter for me.

"She really was talking about me, wasn't she,
Abby?"

"Who knows, C.J. The woman tells lies for a living."

"She said I was flaky. Do you think I am?"

"You're fanciful," I said, choosing the word carefully. "Pie crusts are flaky. There is a big difference."

"And she insulted your shop, Abby. Shall I ask her to leave?"

"No, maybe the ghost will get her."

"Ooh, you're bad, Abby."

The doorbell rang.

The next Hustler to arrive was Thelma Maypole, who looked nothing like a maypole. I knew from Mama that Ms. Maypole was a retired investments counselor, but if I'd had to guess an occupation, I would have said food-taster at Shoney's breakfast bar, and that the woman loved her job.

The large woman was conservatively dressed, had short gray hair cropped in a blunt wedge. She sported the first pair of hexagonal spectacles I'd ever seen. When we shook hands I was reminded that I needed to schedule a mammogram.

"I hope you didn't have any trouble finding my house," C.J. said.

Thelma Maypole peered through her poly-sided lenses. "I did have a bit of trouble. Mozella said you lived directly opposite Colonial Lake. You actually live two thirds of the way down, if you're coming from the northwest, but one third up, of course, if you're coming from the southeast. Even those distances are only approximate."

"I'll make a note of that," C.J. said cheerfully.

Thelma Maypole was not finished. "Did you know that Colonial Lake was formed in 1768 as a marina for the leisure class? Hitherto, this part of town was marsh. You see, the plantation owners—"

Although not particularly religious, I said a prayer of thanksgiving when the doorbell rang again. "I'll get that," I said, and scurried past the hostess.

It was my fault. I should have let C.J. answer her own door. But how was I to know that the next pair of Hustlers were just that. Hustlers. Mama had cagily withheld some pertinent facts—most important of which were Hugh and Sondra Riffle's names. All she'd said was that they were used-car dealers.

Hugh and Sondra Riffle *are* used-car dealers—but used-car dealers with an edge. They only sell cars that once belonged to famous people. Want to buy the '54 Chevy where your favorite rock star lost his or her virginity? Hugh and Sondra have it. Or did your favorite movie star end his or her life in a '69 Ford, a rubber hose funneling the toxic fumes from the exhaust into the front seat? Maybe even an automobile that had seen a grisly wreck. Don't worry, the Riffles have those cars as well. Cars of the Stars, they call their business.

You may think that Charleston, South Carolina, is an odd place for a celebrity-related business to flourish, but the peninsula south of Broad Street does, in fact, contain the fifth-highest concentration of wealth in the country. And, of course, we get tourists from all over. You'd be surprised how many folks fly in to the Lowcountry, as we call our coastal counties, and drive out in a car in which somebody famous has either died, had an orgasm, or otherwise left behind some DNA.

I'd seen the Riffle ads on local television, and they were as tasteless as the concept itself. Hugh Riffle is a blocky ex-linebacker with a face like a side of raw beef. Sondra is a former beauty queen, whose heart-shaped face has seen one too many facelifts. She looks perpetually surprised, although perhaps that's intentional on her part. I had the feeling that underneath her much-tightened exterior was a brain of no small dimensions.

Hugh was dressed in white slacks and a blue short-sleeve shirt, open halfway to the waist. He didn't have a whole lot of chest hair to show off, but the gold chain I saw was thick enough to tether an elephant. Sondra wore a white silk pantsuit and surprisingly little jewelry. Sure, she had a wedding band, and a diamond engagement ring the size of an acorn, but the only other bauble she wore was a brightly colored enameled frog pin on her lapel. She wasn't even wearing earrings. Even her shoes—while nice— didn't cost a fortune.

"What a lovely house," she said, stepping into C.J.'s foyer. "Georgian, isn't it?"

"That's right." She had extended her hand to be

shaken, and I did so slowly. You can tell more by a woman's hands than her face. These hands hadn't waved to a runway audience in decades. Still, she had a firm grip.

Hugh Riffle, on the other hand, had a surprisingly lax shake. I felt like I was holding a boneless chicken breast.

"You Miss Cox?" he asked. "This your house?"

"I'm Abigail Washburn. I'm Jane's friend."

His left brow shot up.

"Not that kind of friend. But if I was, so what? Do you have a problem with that?"

"Not at all, little lady. Sondra here swings both ways—if you get my drift."

"I think I'm getting your draft," I said, and letting go of the boneless chicken breast, scooted around him to greet the next guest on C.J.'s behalf.

Something interesting was coming up the walk.

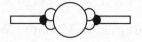

4

Madame Woo-Woo looked like the carnival caricature of a gypsy fortune-teller. She wore layers of orange, purple, and hot pink ruffled skirts, a white peasant blouse, and a lime-green polyester scarf. The cheap gold-tone hoops that hung from stretched earlobes were big enough for a basketball. Her hair was dyed an impossible shade of black and her lipstick was the color of fresh blood. My first impulse was to laugh.

"Good-evening," I said. Southern girls are bred to suppress their impulses. "You must be Madame Woo-Woo."

She extended a gnarled hand with nails as black as my ex-husband's heart. "And you are Abigail Washburn."

"I am? I mean, I *am*! But how did you know?"

Madame Woo-Woo wrapped her other set of ebony claws around my hand. She gazed fixedly into my eyes. I wasn't sure, but in the dim light of C.J.'s gas lantern, it appeared as if Madame Woo-Woo's peepers were baby blue.

"Mrs. Washburn—Mrs. Wiggins Timberlake Washburn—you have the healthiest aura I have ever seen."

"I do?"

She leaned close enough for me to confirm her eye color. I also confirmed that she had eaten curry for supper.

"You are entering what I like to call the golden age of your life—"

"But I'm not even fifty," I wailed.

"Bah!" She expectorated on C.J.'s verandah floor. "The senior years are not so golden. But you—you are now in the prime of your life. Your children—Susan and Charlie, yes?—are doing well in college, and you have a new husband, and a new house south of Broad Street."

"How do you know all this?"

"Madame Woo-Woo knows everything, Mrs. Washburn—well, almost everything. I wish I'd known about the stock market slump of 2001." She chortled briefly. "But of course you didn't need to worry about that. And business for you, by the way, is going to exceed your expectations this year."

"It is?"

"Without a doubt. The planets are aligned in your favor this year. In fact, they haven't been in such a lucrative position—for you, I mean—in decades. But you will need to act fast. There," she said, and although she hadn't moved her hands from mine, I could feel a card pressing into my palm. "This is my private number. Call anytime for a complete evaluation of your future. The card also allows for a twenty percent discount." The talons pressed harder. "Why don't we just set up a meeting for, say, ten o-clock tomorrow morning?"

"Well, I—uh—"

"Mrs. Washburn, I know for a fact that you are a brilliant businesswoman. You would be a fool to pass up this once in a lifetime opportunity. And you are anything but a fool, Mrs. Washburn. Am I correct?"

Before I could think of a clever rejoinder, Madame Woo-Woo whooshed past me, swirling her taffeta skirts. It was time to greet the next guest.

Dr. Francis Lloyd Whipperspoonbill was a letdown after Madame Woo-Woo. He wore a blue and white seersucker suit, which is the summer uniform of adult male native Charlestonians and longterm residents. His bald pate reflected C.J.'s gas light, but what little hair the doctor had was short and neatly combed. He spoke in a cultured voice, but softly, and through clenched teeth. It was obvious that the man was used to having people listen when he spoke.

"Welcome Dr. Whippersnapper—I mean spoonbill!"

He ignored my gaff, and pointed to the dress he'd supplied. "It fits very nice."

"Thank you, sir."

"You're Mozella's daughter, aren't you?"

"Guilty."

"I beg your pardon?"

"Yes, I'm Mozella Wiggins's daughter, Abigail. I'm a close friend of Jane Cox, the hostess. Won't you please come in?"

He seemed hesitant. "Are the others here?"

"All but one, the real estate agent, I believe."

"Ah yes, our honorary Hustler. Well, Chiz is always late."

"Chiz?"

"Chisholm Banncock IX. Chiz we call the young one in each generation."

"So you're a native Charlestonian, Doctor?"

"Three hundred years," he said. At least that's what I think he said. He spoke so low he might well have said "three hungry years."

At any rate, two centuries is the minimum length of time one's ancestors have to have resided in Charleston, in order to qualify someone as a native—although three centuries is obviously much better. Any pedigree that does not extend from before the Late Unpleasantness, and one might as well be "from off." As in "from off" yonder; Kalamazoo, Katmandu, or any place in between.

Generally the topic of origins is something the natives bring up on their own—usually within the first five minutes of a conversation. Believe me, there is no need to volunteer one's "offness." "Who are your people?" in some version or another, is probably the first question a newcomer is asked.

By foolishly broaching the subject myself, I deserved to feel like an outsider. But much to my surprise, Dr. Whipperspoonbill appeared to be too much of a gentleman to put me on the spot. Gratefully, I ushered him inside.

"Well," I said, "as soon as Chiz gets here we can get started."

"Did I hear my name spoken in vain?"

I whirled. Standing in the open door behind me was the handsomest man I'd ever seen—besides my husband Greg, of course.

Chiz deserved his nickname. His face had the chiseled look of a classic Roman statue. As a married woman I shouldn't notice such a thing, but his body was chiseled as well. His pecs strained against the expensive micro-fiber shirt, and his thighs bulged within the confines of tight chinos. And while I'm being frank, that's not all that bulged there. In short, he looked like something from off the cover of a romance novel—he even had dark curly hair and dimples!

I couldn't believe neither C.J. nor my mother had warned me—although no warning was necessary, mind you. Still, given that C.J. and Mama are both as man-hungry as sharks, it was a wonder they hadn't drowned me with drool just mentioning him. For the record, I was utterly unaffected by his maleness—er, his presence.

"You already know who I am," he said with a grin that revealed perfect, white teeth. "Care to clue me in on who you are?"

"Abigail Timberlake!" I cried. "No, I mean Washburn."

The dimples danced. "Washburn Timberlake. Hmm—Washburn is an interesting name for a pretty thing like you. I'm assuming it's a family name."

"It certainly is," a voice from behind me said. "It's her *married* name."

"Mama," I growled. I smiled at Chiz. "Well, now that you're here, we can start."

Chisholm Banncock IX was in no apparent hurry to go anywhere. "Cool duds," he said giving me the once over. "Say, didn't I try to sell you a house?"

"No."

"You sure?"

"Positive." My real estate agent had been a rotund little man with enough hair in his ears to stuff a mattress.

"Well, you look familiar. Where are you from?"

There it was; the "from off" question. It was one thing to be asked it by the older generation, but for a stud muffin like Chiz—surely they no longer cared about such things. I found myself unusually annoyed.

"Two minutes," I said.

"I beg your pardon?"

"It took you two minutes—less, in fact—for you to ask where I'm from."

Chiz grinned. "I hope that's not against the law."

"No, but it ought to be—unless you're asking Yankees. For your information, I was born and raised in South Carolina. Mama, isn't that right?"

"You're still from off, dear," Mama whispered. "Give it up."

Chiz's grin widened. "What was that?"

"She said you shouldn't ask someone where they're from, if all you're trying to do is make a point."

"I said no such thing, Abby."

I ignored my petite progenitress. "Okay, what she really said is it's time for us to go inside and get started. Unless, of course, you're afraid of coming inside."

"Why would I be afraid? I sold Miss Cox this house."

"Exactly. So you know all about the Apparition American. You're probably afraid of coming face to face with her at the séance."

"I am not."

I flapped elbows to simulate chicken wings. "Buck buck brat!"

"Abby," Mama pleaded, "be good."

I could feel myself blush. I had been flirting shamelessly, and my mother knew it. The only way for me to save face was to accept my own challenge and head inside.

Madame Woo-Woo was one tough fortunetelling cookie. She insisted on assigning seats. She put drop-dead gorgeous Chiz on her left, and then continuing the clockwise pattern, seated Ella Nolte, Hugh Riffle, C.J., Mama, Sondra Riffle, Thelma Maypole, myself, and to my left, Dr. Francis Lloyd Whipperspoonbill.

Earlier she'd had C.J. light four candles and place them in the approximate corners of the room, before turning off the lights. In the center of the table Madame Woo-Woo herself had placed an inverted water glass. Except for the cassette recorder, those were the only props of which I was aware.

"Let us begin," Madame Woo-Woo said in a clear, strong voice.

"And with Thy Spirit," Mama responded. She is, after all, a devout Episcopalian.

We had not yet been told to close our eyes, and I could see Madame Woo-Woo scowl. She cleared her throat as a warning.

"There is to be no speaking—except for myself, of course. Mediums are allowed to speak. And our honored guest, if that is what she wishes."

"Yes, ma'am," Mama said, thoroughly chastised.

But even that was too much for Madame Woo-Woo. She turned to C.J.

"This woman will have to leave!"

C.J. may be my best friend, but she and Mama are as close as bone and gristle. The poor girl was mortified.

"Mozella is sorry. Aren't you, Mozella?"

"I didn't do anything wrong," Mama sniffed.

"You spoke," Thelma Maypole said.

I gave Thelma the evil eye. "You just now spoke as well."

"Enough!" Madame Woo-Woo leaped to her sandaled feet, knocking her chair over behind her.

I don't think any of us was fooled by this theatrical display. We sat quietly, but unrepentant, and in a moment Madame Woo-Woo settled her voluminous and hideously colored skirts back on C.J.'s Chippendale-style captain's chair.

"Now close your eyes," she barked.

I closed mine just enough to give the appearance they were shut. At times like these it helps to have long lashes and wear lots of mascara. I had no trouble peeking through the slats, and what I saw pleased me immensely; Madame Woo-Woo's hands disappeared beneath the table.

A second later she began to moan. She sounded just like my ex did in the bathroom every time he ate chili dogs. It was all I could do to not suggest she try Pepto-Bismol.

The moaning stopped abruptly. "I find myself unable to channel tonight," Madame Woo-Woo announced. "I am going to have to speak to the spirit directly."

Having learned our lessons, we said nothing.

"Open your eyes," Madame Woo-Woo ordered.

We opened them—or opened them wider, as the case may be. It was clear to me what the fickle fortune-teller was doing. It was all just part of her act, a ploy to build up the drama.

She made it a point to look each of us in the eye before continuing. "Contacting a spirit directly involves risk. They're not always benevolent, no matter what those mediums on TV say. If the spirit demands a certain course of action, we are obliged to comply. Otherwise we risk paying the consequences. Before I continue, are they any questions?"

Hugh Riffle, who sold dead celebrities' cars for a living, had the pallor of cottage cheese. "What sort of consequences?"

Madame Woo-Woo's forehead formed furrows so deep I heard the melodic tones of Mandarin emanating from one of them. She stared at the glass in the center of the table.

"Some spirits have such strong presence that, when they get really angry, they have the power to take another back with them into their realm."

Sondra Riffle gasped. "You mean, like kill someone?"

Ella Nolte rolled her eyes. "Why, that's just ridiculous. Ghosts—if they exist—are just confused souls who haven't realized yet that they're dead. They're not out to get anyone. In my latest book, *Give Us This Day Our Daily Dead*, I have a character—"

Madame Woo-Woo's glare cut Ella Nolte's self-promotion short. "Enough! You are wasting my time. The spirit's time too."

"I should think the spirit has more than enough time on her bony hands." I clamped a petite paw over my maw. I couldn't believe I'd said that.

Madame Woo-Woo was on her feet again, her chair tipped on its back on the floor. "There will be no séance."

"I'm sorry!" I cried. "I really am!"

"Ooh, ooh, please don't go!" C.J. was beside herself. It was she, after all, who had to live with the Apparition American on a daily basis.

Madame Woo-Woo was far too angry to shoot mere daggers at us. She shot full-length hari-kari swords, daring us to eviscerate ourselves if we said another word. We hung our heads in shame and closed our eyes again.

"Very well," she growled. "I will give it one last try. But if I hear one word"—she paused to toss me another sword—"I'm out of here. Is that understood?"

We nodded mutely. At last, the séance could begin.

5

I peaked again through lacquered lashes. Sure enough, Madame Woo-Woo's black claws were sliding under the table. She cleared her throat.

"Oh resident spirit, please come forth and make your presence known."

My heart was pounding so hard that I didn't hear the windstorm begin. Perhaps the others did. But when Sarah MacGregor began to speak, Thelma Maypole started with such a jolt that her hexagonal glasses slid to the tip of her stubby nose.

"My God, what was that!" Ella Nolte was more afraid of the spirit than she was of our cranky medium.

Madame Woo-Woo had impressive reflexes. She stopped the tape after just four words.

"There is no need to be afraid," she said, in a voice as soothing as chamomile tea. "We have made contact, that's all."

"I heard a woman's voice, but I didn't hear what she said." Hugh Riffle still had his eyes closed, but he looked tense, ready to bolt.

Thinking that no one could see her, Madame Woo-Woo was grinning from ear to bangled ear. "The spirit said her name is Sarah MacGregor. I will ask her now to identify herself further." She took a deep, theatrical breath before continuing. "Sarah MacGregor, please tell us more about yourself."

Several seconds elapsed. "I am mistress of this house. Who, pray tell, are you?"

"My name is Madame Woo-Woo. Think of me as a bridge, Sarah MacGregor—between you and the world you left behind."

"But I did not invite you here. I must insist that you leave."

"I understand how you feel, Ms. MacGregor, but your house—this house—now belongs to someone else. You may not be aware of it, but you have passed over. It is time for you to let go, and get on with the next stage of your existence. I'm sure this is disturbing news, but I don't know how else to put it."

"Tell her she's dead!" C.J. slumped in her chair, to avoid detection. It was as futile as trying to hide a horse in one's pocketbook.

Madame Woo-Woo glared at the big gal. "As I was saying, Ms. MacGregor, it is time for you to complete the crossing."

"This is *my* house," Sarah MacGregor said in her thick, uneven burr. "I will not leave. It is you who must do so."

"Perhaps if we gave you a gift, you would let us stay a short while longer."

"What sort of gift?"

"How about money?"

"Yes, a gift of money would be very nice. The repairs on this home are outrageous."

"Hmm, it just occurred to me, Ms. MacGregor, that giving you a gift of money might be a trifle difficult. You see, we are from another time—wait, I've got it! There is one among us, more sensitive than the others, who could collect the donations and deliver them to you."

"Aye, there is one among ye that seems more sensitive than most. Her name is"—Sarah MacGregor's voice rose slightly, but her Scottish accent improved—"her name is Jane Cox. She's the big girl sitting over there—"

"What the hell!" Madame Woo-Woo's head disappeared beneath the table. She surfaced a second or two later, her face as white as Casper's.

"Is there anything wrong?" Sarah MacGregor asked, her accent by now much improved.

"Nothing is wrong," the medium barked. She glared at me. "This séance is over."

Sarah MacGregor was as stubborn as her Highland forbears. "Nay, I shall not be dismissed like this. I demand that you and your minions leave at once."

"Silence!"

"Nay!"

Madame Woo-Woo dumped her chair for the third time. The séance was over.

"Incredible!" Dr. Whipperspooonbill may have been one of the old guard, but he was not above talking with a ham biscuit in his mouth.

"If I hadn't heard it with my own ears," Ella Nolte said, "I wouldn't have believed it. You can bet this is going to end up in one of my books."

Hugh Riffle took a sip of the cheap red wine C.J. had provided. It seemed to suit him, because he immediately took another.

"I wonder," he mused, "if it's possible to find out how this MacGregor woman died."

"She died in a carriage accident," I said wickedly. "Last I heard the family still owns it. They have it stored in a garage somewhere."

"Do you think they'd sell it?"

Before I could come up with a clever quip, Thelma Maypole grabbed me by an elbow and steered me to the far corner of C.J.'s drawing room. The hexagonal glasses reflected the lights from the overhead chandelier, making her look like she had a head full of fireflies.

"You're not fooling anyone with this nonsense," she hissed. "I know that was you on the tape, at the end. And that last thing you said—that wasn't even taped. I saw your lips move."

"Busted."

"Mrs. Washburn, we of the Heavenly Hustlers are a sophisticated and cultured group. We don't normally attend séances. I personally agreed to come only as a favor to your mother, whom, I might add, is just a bit too eccentric to fit in."

"*What*? You think my mother is too eccentric for your silly little club? Why just look at your—"

My guardian angel must have usurped Madame Woo-Woo's body for a second, because the medium's black claws dug into my other elbow and I was pulled across the room to the opposite corner, before I could shoot my mouth off. Unfortunately, my angel didn't stick around.

"What the hell was that all about?" the real Madame Woo-Woo demanded.

"Ms. Maypole and I were talking investments. What do you think about the recent stock market swing? Is this a good time to sell?"

"I meant what were you trying to pull back there at the table?"

"Oh, you must be referring to the tape incident. The one you rigged under the table."

"Mrs. Washburn, telling fortunes and conducting séances is what I do for a living. Illusion is part of my job."

"Oh, is that what they call it these days? I call it swindling—no, I call it extortion. You threatened dire consequences if folks didn't pay up."

She took a step forward into my comfort zone, her

ruffles brushing my knees. "You're one to talk. You sell used furniture at a premium."

"That's different. Antiques have an intrinsic value. In fact, most of them are better made than contemporary pieces. And besides, I don't threaten my customers. You know, Madame Woo-Woo—or whatever your real name is—I have half a mind to turn you over to the authorities. I'm sure the police can find some charge to stick you with, and if they can't— well, I'm sure the Better Business Bureau will be all ears."

"You little bitch!"

She said it loud enough so that all eyes, including Ms. Maypole's myriad orbs, turned on us. I felt like the time I went down the water slide up in Fort Mill, wearing my yellow and white polka dot bikini, and my bottom piece stayed behind. *That* was a wax job gone to waste, if ever there was one.

"Please," I whispered, "can't we take this outside?"

Instead of doing me the courtesy of answering, Madame Woo-Woo swayed like a long leaf pine in a hurricane. Then, like most of the pines during Hugo, she toppled over.

Mama called 911. In the meantime, Sondra Riffle, who knew CPR, and was convinced Madame Woo-Woo had suffered a heart attack, tried to revive the medium. Dr. Francis Lloyd Whipperspoonbill, it turned out, had been trained as a veterinarian, not a people doctor. Thanks to Sondra's efforts, Madame Woo-Woo was still alive when the paramedics arrived, and since C.J. lives practically within the shadow of the Medical University of South Carolina, there appeared to be hope.

"She landed right on top of me," I said to Sergeant Scrubb, without looking directly at him.

The detective, whom I'd had the privilege of meeting on a prior occasion, is a dead ringer for Ben Affleck. Normally, I find it hard not to look at Sergeant Scrubb. Heck, I've even fantasized about him—well, never mind about that. My husband Greg was in the room with us, and even though he still smelled like raw shrimp, he was all I had eyes for. Besides, I was in enough trouble as it was.

"But you weren't hurt?"

"My hoops deflected some of the impact."

"Thank God for that," Greg said.

"Some of the others reported that you and"— Sergeant Scrubb consulted his notes—"Golda Feinstein were involved in a dispute."

"Golda Feinstein! Madame Woo-Woo's real name is Golda Feinstein?"

"According to the authoress, Ella Nolte, who seems to know her best."

"Author."

"Ma'am?"

"I think they call them just authors these days. I mean, you don't hear anyone say 'engineeress,' do you? Or 'detectivess.' Now that would be just plain silly, wouldn't it?"

Sergeant Scrubb looked to Greg for help. My beloved merely smiled and shrugged.

The cute detective sighed. "Back to the matter of this alleged dispute, Abby. What can you tell me about it?"

"It wasn't a dispute exactly. She was just pissed—pardon my French—because I almost exposed her as a fraud."

"How do you mean?"

"No one told you?"

He started to shake his handsome head, but caught himself. The end result is that he cocked his head, which made him all the cuter.

"Suppose you tell me," he said.

"Well, tell your forensics team to get down on their hands and knees because there's a tiny little cassette recorder taped to the underside of the dining room table. Madame Woo-Woo used it as a prop, to make her customers think she was communicating with a ghost. And yes, that is my voice on there as well, because, you see, I found the recorder before the séance and decided to give the medium a dose of her own medicine."

Greg grinned, but said nothing.

"What exactly was her medicine?" Sergeant Scrubb asked.

"Extortion—well, that's what I call it. She was pretending to be a ghost who demanded money. Sounds crazy, doesn't it? I can't imagine anybody falling for that scam. Still, I don't like frauds, so I thought I'd put a stop to it."

Sergeant Scrubb jotted a note or two down on a palm-sized pad of paper. "I know of even crazier scams that have worked. Well, I guess that's it for now, Abby—oh, except for one thing. If you don't mind my asking, why are you and your mother dressed like that?"

I could feel my cheeks redden. "It was Mama's idea. Since the real ghost is antebellum, Mama thought she would feel more at home if we dressed in period clothes. Unfortunately, Mama and I were the only two who could fit into them."

"It's a pretty good fit, if you ask me," Greg said with a wink.

I felt like an actor who'd forgotten her lines and had to ad lib. "Would either of you like something to eat? There are still some ham biscuits left, and hardly anyone touched the cake. It's triple layer chocolate, by the way, with double fudge frosting."

"Cake would be nice," Greg said.

We were sitting around a small table in what C.J. planned to turn into a breakfast nook. Originally the space had been a butler's pantry, and there was evidence to suggest it may have started out as an oversized, manually operated lift. Charleston homes are subject to flooding, and many are built a full story off the ground. At any rate, it made a perfect interrogation room, lacking only a naked light bulb to live up to its dramatic potential. The antique ginger-jar lamp C.J. had on the table just didn't cut the mustard.

The cake was sitting on a kitchen counter, just yards away. I got up to get it, but hadn't gone half the distance when Greg leaped to his feet and pulled me around the refrigerator where we couldn't be seen by Sergeant Scrubb.

"Hon," my husband whispered, "I think you're leaking."

"Leaking?"

"You're trailing water—or something."

I turned and looked behind me. Sure enough, a trail of drops glistened on the dark ancient planks of C.J.'s floor.

"Damn! That's all Buford's fault."

"What?" Greg was truly alarmed now. "Do you need to go to the doctor?"

I smiled at the love of my life. He's as dense as ebony, but my welfare is always first and foremost on his mind.

"You see, Mama and I pinned bags of ice inside our skirts, to keep us cool. While we were doing it the subject of Buford came up—he's in town by the way—and I got distracted, and must have pinned one of the bags upside down. You know, with that zip closure on the bottom, instead of on top."

"Abigail Washburn," Greg said folding me into his arms, "you're a mess, but I love you anyway."

"I love you too, you big bucket of bait." No matter how hard my hubby scrubs, he still smells like his work.

We kissed. We didn't exactly get carried away—Greg, for one, disapproves of PDAs—but we did manage to brush up against C.J.'s refrigerator. Incidentally, the big gal is one of those folks who keeps her life on display, held in place by a variety of magnets, most of them freebies. Just from perusing the outside of C.J.'s refrigerator, I could tell that she was adored by an eight-year-old niece named Samantha with a face full of freckles, had a dentist appointment in two weeks, disagreed with the late Ann Landers on wedding etiquette, needed to order more pine straw to use as mulch, was at least thinking about having some spider veins removed, had recently changed insurance companies, owned season tickets to the Dock Street Theatre, and had an inexplicable interest in Viagra.

It was the corn on the cob magnet holding up the newspaper clipping on Viagra that I inadvertently knocked loose. The magnet itself was easy enough to retrieve, but the clipping assumed a life of its own, sailed into the nearest wall, and slid back behind the refrigerator. To make a long story short, my arms were too short to retrieve it, and Greg's too thick.

Therefore, we had no choice but to pull the fridge a few inches away from the wall.

I still say I had no choice but to scream when I saw what else lay behind that ancient avocado green appliance.

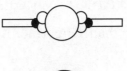

6

"Abby, are you all right!" The concern in Greg's voice was touching.

"I'm fine, but just look at that!"

"Yeah, she should dust behind here sometimes, but that's no cause to shriek. You nearly busted my eardrums."

"It's not the dust bunnies!" I shrieked again, partly out of frustration, and partly just for good measure. "It's the wall behind the fridge."

"What about the wall?" Sergeant Scrubb was peering over my shoulder. He had, of course, joined us by then, as had everyone who was at the pseduo-séance—except for poor Madame Woo-Woo, AKA Golda Feinstein.

"It's not just a wall," I said. It was all I could do not to call him an idiot. "It's the tiles on the wall."

"Frankly, dear," Mama said, "they look ugly to me. I can see why the former owner painted over the rest of them. I would have too, only I would have used some color other than tangerine. Maybe a nice pale peach."

"That paint is a sacrilege," I sputtered. "If my guess is right, those are early seventeenth-century Portuguese tiles. C.J., where do you keep your paper towels? And bring me a little water, would you?"

"Seventeenth century," Mama muttered. "Why that would make them almost three hundred years old."

"More like four hundred," I said. A lot of folks, even some within the antique business, don't seem to understand that the first century wasn't over until one hundred years after the birth of Christ. There seems to have been a lot of millennium confusion as well—although that didn't affect the price of my merchandise. Instead it resulted in an invitation to a bang-up party with a live band and a karaoke machine, not to mention a roast pig with an apple in its mouth. Even though it was a year early, Greg got plastered and sang "House of the Rising Sun" so off key that even the roast pig wept tears of anguish. Either that, or I was inebriated as well.

"Here, Abby." C.J. had trotted over with a two-quart Pyrex bowl filled with fresh water, and a clean dishtowel. I couldn't have asked for better service.

With the crowd pushing around me, and in some cases towering over me, I dipped one end of the cloth in the water and gently dabbed at a tile. Progress, if any, was slow. Untold years of kitchen grease and airborne dust had formed a stubborn film. Even a vigorous scrub with the water-soaked cloth did no good.

"C.J., got any Fantastik?"

She hopped to it. Now, I would never recommend this to my clients, and it was really very foolish on my part, but desperate times call for desperate measures, and I was desperate to prove my point. Besides, I couldn't be positive I was looking at a treasure; there was always the off-chance Mama was right.

I sprayed a small area of one tile, and immediately wiped away the chemicals. To my great joy and amazement, the grime was lifted and the tile appeared undamaged. I worked on the rest of the tile until it gleamed like the day it was first glazed. When I was done, I stepped back—after having to elbow a few people aside—to gaze on my handiwork.

"Not bad," Mama conceded.

"Not bad? It's in perfect condition."

"What's it supposed to be?" Maybe it's his detective training, but Greg has to see the whole picture before he can even venture a guess.

I grabbed the other end of the towel and wiped two more tiles clean. "That's a flower, and there you have part of what looks to be a cherub. See the fat little face and a portion of a wing?"

"Big deal," Ella Nolte grunted. "They're just old tiles, and they aren't particularly well painted."

"These *old* tiles," I said, willing myself to remain calm, "could be worth upwards of three hundred dollars."

Ella snorted. "I paid three hundred dollars for my handbag. Like I said, big deal."

"*Each.*"

"Abby, you're joking!" Mama pushed forward for a better look.

C.J. shook her equine head. "She's not. We've sold individual tiles for that much at the shop, haven't we, Abby?"

"You betcha. And a complete scene—well, we don't know what this wall contains, do we? There could be a fortune under that hideous orange paint."

"Abby," Greg said, his voice full of pride, "you never cease to amaze me. How could you tell by looking at that"—he pointed to a tile in its original state—"you would get this?" He pointed to a clean one. "And how the hell did you know they were Portuguese?"

"I'm not sure they are Portuguese, dear. I'm only guessing at this point. But if you'd paid attention on our honeymoon, you might be able to help me with identification."

"I paid attention to the important stuff, didn't I?" Greg gave my shoulders a squeeze.

We'd honeymooned in Portugal. It was my idea; I'd always had a thing for that Iberian country. I'm not saying I believe in reincarnation, but if did, I'm sure I was Portuguese in a former life. At any rate, I did my homework well before the trip, and once there—when we weren't in our romantic hotels, doing the romantic thing—I dragged my new husband to every museum, palace, and church I could squeeze into the agenda. And of course we did the antique shops.

Many tourists head straight for the beaches of the Algarve, in the south, but both Greg and I found the mountaintop town of Sintra to be the most charming place we'd ever visited; we vowed to return someday for a month's stay. Even busy Lisbon captivated us far more than we'd anticipated, and by the time we hit the National Museum of Azulejo in Lisbon, I too was dragging. But one step inside that fabulous museum, established in the sixteenth-century convent Madre de Deus, and I was energized.

The Portuguese word for wall tile, *azulejo*, probably derives from the Arabic "az-zulaca," meaning "brilliant surface," and the museum is a veritable jewel box. While Greg slumbered on some thoughtfully placed benches, I gazed at the handiwork of Portugal's finest artisans. I learned a little that day as well, but alas, not enough.

"C.J.," I said, "is it all right with you if I come back tomorrow and clean the entire batch?"

"Don't be silly, Abby, of course you may."

"And if I find a safe way," I said pushing my luck, "may I clean that awful orange paint off the rest of them?"

C.J. bit her lower lip. "I kinda like the orange. I was planning to paint pink stripes across it and—" She shook her massive head, and for a second I felt my hopes sink. But the big gal is a pragmatist and, above all, a keen businesswoman. "If you close the shop, Abby, I'll help you strip the paint."

That was going a little too far. I didn't have anything to gain if C.J.'s tiles turned out to be as valuable as I hoped. On the other hand, a closed shop meant lost revenue for me.

"If it's all the same," I said, "I'd rather work alone. You see, I feel the need for solitude coming on."

"That's because her ex-husband is in town," my mini-madre explained to her compadres.

"Mama!"

"But it's true, dear." She turned to the others. "Buford Timberlake is the slime on the ooze on sludge on the muck at the bottom of the pond. I think that's how she put it. Anyway, even though he's the father of my grandchildren, I'd have to agree."

"Dirty linen," I said through gritted teeth.

"What's that, dear?" Mama's hearing ranges from perfect, to just above that of a stone, depending on her mood.

"I think she doesn't want you to air her dirty linens in public," C.J. said in a voice loud enough to wake the dead two counties over. In her defense the girl was just trying to be helpful. Unfortunately she didn't stop there. "Personally though, I could never see the harm in that. Why, my Granny Ledbetter up in Shelby made a fortune airing her dirty linens in public— well, she would have, except that somebody stole her sheets."

"That's nice, dear," Mama said. Like me, she'd heard one too many Shelby stories.

The Heavenly Hustlers, however, were fresh meat. And when Chiz Bannock flexed his dimples at poor C.J. and asked for details—well, I would have aired my entire hamper on the *Today Show* under those circumstances.

"You see," C.J. explained, "it was back in the nineteen forties. Granny had just finished painting the house, and she'd used real sheets to catch the drips— not plastic drop sheets, on account of they didn't have them in those days. Anyway, no sooner did Granny get done painting, when her milk cow, Clarabelle, went into labor. So Granny used the paint-splattered sheets to lay on the barn floor under the calf when it was born. Then, because they were already so dirty, she used them to kneel on in the vegetable garden when she was weeding. And just so y'all know, up in Shelby it isn't like here, where the ground is sandy. Up there it's all red clay, and it doesn't come out of things, no matter how hard you scrub. Why, once when I was a little girl—"

"C.J.," I said gently, "can you please stick to the main story?"

"No problemo, Abby. Where was I?"

"I think you were trying to tell us how your granny's dirty linen almost made her rich."

"Right. Well, try as she might Granny couldn't get the sheets clean. Finally she gave up and just hung them out on the line to dry. Then later that same day this tourist stops by to ask directions to New York City. Now wasn't that silly?"

"That was pretty silly, dear," Mama said agreeably. "As if your poor Granny would know."

"Oh, but she did. Granny knew five different ways to get there. I meant that it was silly the tourist didn't know how to get there."

"The sheets," I hissed. "Get back to the damn sheets."

"Yeah, right. Well, after the tourist left, Granny went back inside. But then later in the day, when it was fixing to rain, she went back out to get the sheets, only they were gone. A couple of months after that, Granny bought a magazine and inside there was a picture of this famous artist standing next to one of his paintings, and it was the same guy who'd asked Granny directions! And guess what? That wasn't really his painting the guy was standing next to, but one of Granny's sheets."

"That was very entertaining," I said in an attempt to wrap things up. "So, how about it, C.J.? Is it okay if I work on the wall alone tomorrow?"

"I guess so, Abby."

"Thanks."

"Wait a minute," Chiz said. "You never told us who the artist was." I wanted to slap the boy—gently, of course—dimples and all.

C.J. giggled. "Well, his first name is the capital of Mississippi and his last name is a type of fish."

"Jackson Pollock did not steal your granny's sheets!" I said irritably.

I had more to say but, fortunately for both of us, Sergeant Scrubb's cell phone rang. He returned to the cramped breakfast nook to take the call. When he emerged a few minutes later, he was frowning.

"Greg, may I see you a minute?"

"Sure," my sweetie said, but when he took his first step in Scrubb's direction, you can bet that the whole bunch of us surged forward with him, like an eight-headed beast.

The detective held up a restraining hand and laughed. "Whoa. Okay, okay, I was going to tell you all the basics anyway, so I may as well do it all at once. That was my partner, Sergeant Bright, on the phone. He was calling from the Medical University of South Carolina." Sergeant Scrubb swallowed. "Golda Feinstein, also known as Madame Woo-Woo, is dead."

"Oh my God!" Sondra Riffle looked genuinely upset.

Her husband, Hugh, put his arm around her. "Did she die in the ambulance?"

"If not," I said, "I'm sure there are a lot of other

ambulances in which folks have died. One of them might be for sale."

He gave me a blank stare.

Thelma Maypole's stare, on the other hand, was anything but blank. The orange light reflecting from the painted tiles, and further distorted by the weird lenses, made her irises look like freshly fanned coals. She fixed the embers on me.

"*If* it really was a heart attack," she said, "we know who is to blame."

"I didn't do anything!" I wailed.

"Yes you did, dear—" Mama clamped a hand over her meddling little mouth.

"It wasn't a heart attack," Sergeant Scrubb said, with a shake of his head. No doubt he'd never seen a bigger bunch of babies outside a Pampers commercial. "I'm not free to—no, I'm *not* going to discuss the details now. But it wasn't a heart attack."

"I get it—" I stopped. Greg was mouthing the words "shut up" to me.

Ella Nolte pushed her way to the front of the pack. "Sergeant Scrubb, there is no need to play games with us. I am a professional writer of mystery novels, and I know what's going on."

"Games!" C.J. said, clapping her hands with glee. "I just love games. Granny and I used to play one called Prussian Roulette."

Mama patted the big gal's arm. "You mean *Russian* Roulette, don't you dear?"

"No, ma'am, I meant Prussian—well, German, at least. You see, Granny would make all these miniature strudels. Most of them she would fill with apple, but every now and then she'd hide a jalapeño in one of them. Then she would divide the pastries between us, and the game was to see who could eat all of theirs without making a face."

Ella Nolte rolled her beady eyes. "Mozella, your young friend here has almost enough imagination to be a writer herself. But even she hasn't guessed what it is the Sergeant refuses to tell us."

"Then you tell us," Mama said. She was practically begging.

The pedantic pen pusher had the figure of a scarecrow built without straw. Nonetheless, she thrust her scrawny chest skyward in a proud gesture and poked the air with a bony finger.

"What he's not telling you is that Madame Woo-Woo was murdered here tonight, and we are all suspects."

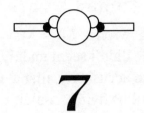

7

We all stared at Sergeant Scrubb.

"Is that true?" I asked. To my credit I remained as calm as Charleston Harbor on those days Greg and I decide to go sailing.

Sergeant Scrubb, on the other hand, could have zipped out of the harbor without tacking once. "I said nothing about murder. I merely said it wasn't a heart attack."

"Oh my God." Ella Norte clapped both hands to her sunken cheeks in an act of pure melodrama. "Madame Woo-Woo was poisoned!"

Sergeant Scrubb started. "How did you know that, ma'am?"

Ella let loose with one of her snorts. "Well, it's not because I'm the guilty party, if that's what you're thinking. But there was food served tonight, wasn't there?"

The strange orange light seemed to go out in Thelma Maypole's eyes. She hugged her ample abdomen, as if she might suddenly be experiencing pain.

"Is something wrong, Miss Maypole?" Sergeant Scrubb asked. He didn't seem unduly concerned.

Thelma looked accusingly, first at C.J., and then at me. "We could all be dying, couldn't we?"

"In a way we all are," I said. "Life is a terminal disease, is it not?"

"That's not what I mean, and you know it." She unwrapped one beefy arm from her middle long enough to point a sausage finger at me. "Mozella Wiggins's daughter—Abigail, I think her name is—played a nasty trick on that poor medium."

Hugh Riffle moved into position, like a linebacker waiting for the referee's whistle. "What sort of nasty trick?"

It was time for me to step up to the scrimmage line. "Madame Woo-Woo had rigged a recorder under the table. Her intent was to get money out of y'all. I merely made that more difficult."

Hugh blinked. "You mean that wasn't a ghost we heard?"

"Bingo."

Ella Nolte snorted again. If she wasn't careful, one of the many carriage tour companies that does business in Charleston's historic district was going to harness that woman and put her to work. Think of the money they'd save, because no doubt Ella could pull the wagon *and* deliver the lecture.

"That's ridiculous," she said. "I felt chills run up and down my arms when the ghost spoke."

"That was probably just C.J.'s air-conditioner. You were sitting under a vent."

"I think all of you are missing the point," Sondra Riffle said. She had the soft sort of voice one might expect from a former, and very much faded, beauty queen. Perhaps because of that, and because she rarely spoke, we paid her our full attention. "Whatever it is that killed Madame Woo-Woo could be killing us right now, only more slowly. Shouldn't we be at the hospital?"

"Why, that was precisely *my* point." Thelma Maypole clutched her stomach even tighter.

"I'll call 911," Mama said brightly. She's always up for a bit of excitement, which is probably why she hooked up with this lively bunch.

"Don't be silly," C.J. said. "911 is standing right there." She nodded at Sergeant Scrubb.

The sergeant, meanwhile, seemed curiously unconcerned. "Why don't we just drive over?"

"I've got room in my car for six," Chiz Banncock volunteered.

"Better make that fast," Ella Nolte grunted. She wrapped her beanpole arms around her nonexistent middle and doubled over in a gesture of pure agony.

"Ella," Sondra said softly. "Are you all right?"

"Hell no! I think I'm going to die." The queen of melodrama staggered over to a kitchen stool, tried to sit, but slid to the floor instead. Her bony frame barely even made a thump.

"Get a goddamn ambulance!" Hugh Riffle roared. His hands now cradled his rather prodigious belly. His normally florid face was the color of skim milk.

"Greg," Sergeant Scrubb said calmly. "May I see you for a minute?"

I took a step in that direction.

"*Alone*," Sergeant Scrubb said, not quite as calm.

While my dearly beloved trotted off for a tête-à-tête with Charleston's finest, the rest of us fell like flies. Both Hugh Riffle and Thelma Maypole made respectable thuds when they hit the hard floor. Dr. Francis Lloyd Whipperspoonbill was too much of an aristocrat to actually go supine, but instead took Ella's stool, where he perched, looking as miserable as an owl in a two-day rain. Chiz, who was both an aristocrat and a studmuffin, managed to hoist himself up on a kitchen counter. There the hunk sat, hunkered over, his face in his hands.

Aging beauty queens, I soon learned by watching Sondra Riffle, lower themselves to the linoleum with grace. Once there, they arrange their clothing in a seductive fashion, fluff their hair with pastel pink nails, and then lay their store-bought cheekbones gently across bronzed arms.

That left just Mama, C.J., and me standing; the three people I cared most about in that room. For a few seconds, as we stood there staring at the victims, and then each other, I felt relieved. Somehow we'd managed to escape the grim reaper. How optimistic of me.

"Ooh," C.J. started to moan. "Ooh, ooh. I think I'm going to die."

"Join the crowd," Ella whinnied from her position on the floor.

C.J. wasted no time accepting the invitation. Never a gentle giant, she threw her five foot, ten inch frame down like it was a sleeping bag and she was preparing for a sleepover.

Even my mini-madre was teetering around in tight circles, in what little free floor space there was. In her hoop skirt she looked like a bowling pin trying to decide if it had been knocked down.

"Mama! Not you, too!"

"I know you think I love your brother Toy more than you, but that isn't so. I always loved you best, dear."

"*Really?*"

"Of course—well, except maybe for the year you turned fourteen. You were an absolute brat."

"Sorry, Mama."

"Don't worry, dear, I forgave you long ago. I want you to promise me one thing though."

"Anything, Mama!" I had yet to feel a single pang.

"Promise you'll bury me with my pearls on. And I want to be buried in that pink and white gingham dress your daddy loved so much. And those new white pumps I bought just for your wedding."

"I promise," I wailed.

Mama steadied herself to look me in the eyes one last time. "Anything you want to say, dear?"

"I love you."

"Anything else?"

I gulped. "It was me who broke that blue carnival glass dish you kept on the coffee table when Toy and I were kids. I blamed it on him because he wouldn't let me ride shotgun with you when we drove to the beach."

"And I have sinned against you as well, Mozella." C.J. has a pleasant enough voice under normal circumstances, but now she sounded like a bullfrog on steroids.

Mama remained stable long enough to demand that her friend elaborate.

"Remember that time we drove up to Cherokee, North Carolina, to gamble in the casinos?"

"What about it?"

"Remember when you asked me to guard your bucket of chips while you went to the bathroom?"

"Yes."

"Remember how when you returned from the bathroom, there didn't seem to be as many chips in the bucket as when you left?"

"You're forgiven, dear," Mama said to our prostrate hostess. She turned to me. "That blue dish was my mama's, Abby. It was the only thing of hers I had."

"Sorry!"

"I guess sorry will have to do—under the circumstances. Well, good-bye, dear." Mama closed her eyes
and began a slow slump. One by one the hoops in her
skirt collapsed, until she was in a sitting position.
Then with a deft flip she reoriented the hoops in a
vertical position while she lay back on the floor. The
effect was that I could see up Mama's skirts.

I gasped. My mother was wearing pants! Blue
jeans to be exact. And what's more, they seemed to
fit, which meant they couldn't be mine. How could
that be? The woman had never worn pants a day in
her life. Even when we climbed Crowder's Mountain,
a rocky peak to the west of Charlotte, she'd worn a
skirt—with crinolines!

"Mama!" I cried. "Where did you get those jeans?"

She raised her petite gray head and opened one
eye. "At the Gap, dear. Where else?"

"But you never—" I grabbed my side. It suddenly
felt like I had a moray eel swimming up my small in-
testine. I hadn't felt such excruciating pain since giving birth to my daughter Susan. With my son,
Charlie, you can bet I used an epidural.

"Abby!" Greg strode back into the kitchen just as
my knees buckled. His strong hands grabbed me and
stood me back on my feet. The second he let go of
me, I collapsed again.

"Good-bye, darling," I murmured, as I sank into a
heap of hoops and hemlines. "I love you."

Greg, who is every bit as handsome as Rhett But-

ler, scooped me up in his arms and carried me into
C.J.'s living room. But instead of spreading me gently
on a comfortable sofa, he propped me up on a
straight-backed side chair.

"Abby, I've got something to tell you." They say
confession is good for the soul, and being only a
nominal Episcopalian, mine could use all the help it
could get.

"Me too, dear. Remember last Sunday when you
thought you'd flown me to the moon three times?
Well, I only made it there once."

Even though my vision was dimming in death, I
could see Greg blush. "I faked it one of those times
too, hon," he said, "but what I wanted to tell is that
you're not dying."

"Yes, I am. Just behind your head I see the light."

Greg turned and looked up. "That's C.J.'s chandelier. And anyway, you weren't poisoned."

"Of course I was. We all were." Although I must
admit, despite the agonizing pain in my gut, the rest
of me was feeling pretty chipper. It was hard to imagine how I was supposed to accomplish "letting go"
and "floating to the light." Perhaps I'd receive depar-
ture instructions. In the meantime, I would take advantage of my strength, to speak my peace. "Greg, I
want you to know that these few months we've been
married have been among the happiest days of my
life. And I'm sorry I nagged you about leaving the
toilet seat up and dropping your socks and skivvies

just any old where. I'm also sorry I threw your swim-suit edition of *Sports Illustrated* in the garbage, al-though now that you won't have me, it's perfectly all right for you to retrieve it. There are a few things, however, you still might want to keep in mind—"

Greg covered my mouth firmly, but gently, with one of his huge hands. It smelled of raw shrimp and assorted fish culled from his daily catch.

"Abby, please listen. I don't think you were poi-soned because in the phone call Scrubb got from the hospital, the attending physician told him that while Madame Woo—uh, Miss Feinstein—died of respira-tory failure, there was no apparent sign of gastro-nomic distress."

"Mmmb, mmmb, mmmmmmb." Even I couldn't tell what I was saying.

"So you see, Abby, it wasn't something y'all ate. The doc made it plain that he is just guessing at this point, but he thinks it may have been a spider. Possi-bly a black widow."

"Mmb mmb?"

"It could have happened at C.J.'s house. The spider might have been under the table—"

"Mmb!"

"More likely she was bitten by something earlier in the evening. Spider venom often takes a couple of hours to work its way through the blood stream. There weren't any bite marks that the doc could see. Black widows like to hang out between sofa cushions and under toilet seats, so the groin area seems to be the most common target. Doc said Miss Feinstein's groin—"

I may be tiny, but adrenaline is a powerful thing. I ripped Greg's hand away from my mouth.

"TMI!" I cried. I sat forward on the straight-backed chair. Thank heavens it didn't have any cushions.

Greg grinned. "I knew that would get to you. How are you feeling, Hon?"

I took a few seconds to consider. "Surprisingly, I feel much better."

"That pain in your gut all gone?"

"Yes, but what about all those people in there?" The moaning and groaning coming from C.J.'s kitchen made it sound like the setting of an old Boris Karloff movie. It wouldn't surprise me to learn that the resident apparition—whatever her real name was—packed her ectoplasm bags and skedaddled. I sure the heck wouldn't hang out in all that commotion, given the option.

"We've called for two ambulances—just to be on the safe side. They should be here any minute. But what we suspect is happening out there is nothing more than mass hysteria."

"Say what?"

"Mass hysteria. You see it on the news every now and then. Some office worker starts feeling lousy—blames it on fumes—and the next thing you know the whole building is being evacuated. The imagination is a powerful thing."

"Oh God," I moaned.

"Abby, you're not feeling sick again, are you?"

"No, I'm feeling like a fool."

Greg kissed the top of my head. "Well, you're my fool, and you always will be."

"Thanks—I think."

We heard the sirens.

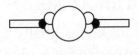

8

To hear Mama tell it, having one's stomach pumped is worse than childbirth. C.J., who'd never given birth, compared it to a root canal. I have a feeling they were both exaggerating, but a tube down one's nose cannot be fun. On the way down, their respective tubes met with a bit of resistance, the result of which was that neither woman felt much like talking for a while.

I excused C.J. from work, and she came and stayed with us for two nights. The second day I caught the two of them laughing so hard I feared for my upholstery. Then it was back to work for the big gal, and back to the assorted bosoms of her compadres for my madre.

In case you're wondering, not one of the Heavenly Hustlers had had a legitimate case of food poisoning. Or any other poison for that matter—unless you count the alcohol level in Hugh Riffle's blood. It's a darn good thing he hadn't breathed too close to any of the candles in the room that fateful night.

At any rate, with things finally back to normal, I took a day off to work on C.J.'s tiles. I went prepared, toting my own cleaning supplies—paint remover, a mild detergent, soft towels—and a book on Portuguese tiles. I didn't plan to use the paint remover without first testing it on a very small area, perhaps no larger than that occupied by my former husband's heart, if seen in cross section.

C.J. and I have keys to each other's houses. When I let myself in, just as calmly as if I owned that house, I noticed that one of the neighbors was just a wee bit too busy sweeping her front steps. I know that virtually every neighborhood has its Gladys Kravitz, so I smiled at the woman and said hello. Her response was to turn an expensively upholstered back.

I stepped inside a house that was as dark as a stack of black cats. Because I am a firm believer in the existence of Apparition Americans, and because I am adverse to stubbing my stubby toes, the first thing I did was to turn on all the downstairs lights. I started with the foyer and proceeded to the living room, then the formal dining room—site of the aborted séance—and ended with the kitchen. When I flipped on that last switch—I wasn't going to bother with the minuscule breakfast nook—I let out a long, loving sigh. Works of art, especially rare antiquities, deserve a little veneration.

But something was wrong. My eyes were refusing to cooperate. Since I hadn't come near anything mind-altering since the early nineteen seventies, I could only blame it on the light—or lack thereof. C.J., like Mama, belongs to the school of thought that favors low wattage and ruined eyes, over high energy consumption. This, however, was ridiculous. I couldn't even see the damn tiles. The fridge had been pushed back in place, of course, but the outline of the other tiles should have been visible through the orange paint.

I rubbed my eyes, and when that didn't work, I tugged at the bottom lids. That little trick has been known to help me focus when alternating between TV and a good mystery by Edie Claire. Alas, my ocular orbs were obstinate, and all I could see was a flat orange wall. I ran to the wall and traced it with desperate fingers, searching for any indentation, as if I were a mountain climber on a sheer rock face. Nada. That wall was as smooth as a politician's tongue.

"What the heck?" I pulled the refrigerator away from the wall. The space behind it was also smooth. And *clean*. Where were all the dirty tiles?

I hoisted my petite patooty up on the nearest bar stool to think. I don't think with my patooty by the way—it's just that my knees were feeling a little weak. There were just two possibilities as I saw it; I'd only dreamed that there were antique Portuguese tiles on C.J.'s kitchen wall, or I was dreaming now.

In the old days one needed to pinch oneself to see if one was awake, but today all one needs is a cell phone. I dug into my bag, extracted a device barely larger than a walnut, and called Greg on his shrimp boat. He picked up on the second ring.

"Abby? What's wrong? Never mind, I'll be right there. I'm turning the boat around as we speak. I can be there in two hours."

"Greg, darling, I'm not hurt. And you don't even know where I am—"

"You're at C.J.'s, hon." I could barely hear my beloved over the sound of his diesel engines and a myriad of gulls. "Wow! But that's just a lucky guess. So I am at C.J.'s. Was I here two nights ago as well? And did I accidentally happen to discover a wall full of antique Portuguese tiles?"

"Hon, you've already made your point on that score. Why are you trying to rub it in?"

"I'm not! Just tell me, dear, 'yes' or 'no.' Were there antique tiles on C.J.'s kitchen wall?"

"You know there were." Despite the background noise, Greg sounded pissed.

"Greg, please just humor me. What's my middle name?" For some strange reason, in my dreams it is always Elizabeth.

"Your middle name is Louise. Abby, what the hell is going on?"

My middle name *is* Louise. I slipped off the stool, staggered over to the wall, and touched it one last time.

"Greg," I said in a voice as piercing as any gull's, "then C.J.'s been robbed."

"Robbed? Abby, it sounded like you said 'robbed.'"

"That is what I said. And you'll never guess what was stolen."

"Some of the tiles?"

"More like the entire wall—well, not the wallboard itself, but every single one of the tiles is gone. And not only that, whoever did it painted the blank wall orange again."

"Abby, are you by yourself?"

"Yeah. C.J.'s running the shop and Mama is off gallivanting."

"Then listen to me very carefully, hon. Get out of the house now."

"Well, I'm not planning to hang around, but I was at least going to call the police first."

"Don't. Get out now."

"Greg, the paint is dry. The tile thief is long gone."

"You don't know that. Perps often really do return to the scene of the crime. I want you to start moving right now—calmly—and just head right on out the door. You hear me?"

"I hear you." I also heard heavy footsteps on the ceiling above me. My blood turned the temperature of a good martini, and I was out of there like a scalded dog.

I called the police, and while I waited for them to come, I called on Mrs. Kravitz. She was still intently sweeping her steps, which by that point, could have passed the white glove test. At any rate, I had to speak twice before she looked at me.

"Can I help you?" she finally asked. She held her broom in front of her, both hands gripping the handle, as if it were a lance.

"My name is Abigail Washburn. Mrs. Abigail Washburn. I'm a friend of your neighbor, Jane Cox. I was wondering if you happened to see anything unusual over there the last couple of days."

"Unusual?"

"Well, like people coming in and out."

Gladys Kravitz had a round chin the size and color of a marshmallow—and I don't mean the miniature kind. She pointed it upward in disdain. "There are always people coming and going over there. You should know, you're one of them."

"Yes, but I specifically mean in the last two days."

She lowered the chin in order to make eye contact. "Nobody in the last two days. But that bunch that was there the night of the ambulance—well, you'd think they lived there."

I smiled patiently. "That's not quite the case, ma'am. Only the fake gypsy—Madame Woo-Woo—had been there before."

"Are you calling me a liar?"

"No ma'am!" Then I remembered Mama. "Well, my mother has been there. She was the other one in the hoop skirt."

"Ah, her. She's the ringleader."

"I beg your pardon?"

Gladys Kravitz didn't appear to be convinced of my innocence. "You're not from here, are you?"

"I'm from 'off,' " I cried. "But I live here now. Besides, what does where I was born have to do with this?"

The chin inched skyward. "Mrs. Wiggins, here in Charleston we require building permits before remodeling."

"Even in 'off' we require building permits. What has this to do with my mother?"

"She's the one who lets the others in. Always when Miss Cox isn't home, of course. She must be the contractor."

"A contractor in crinolines? I'm sorry Mrs. Kravitz—uh, whoever you are. But this doesn't make a lick of sense. Can you start at the beginning?"

Her grasp on the broom relaxed as she began to grasp that I was truly clueless. "Well, it all started about a month ago when your mother and her friends started showing up on a regular basis. Like I said, they come when Miss Cox isn't home. They always come dressed for work—even your mother."

"Get out of town!"

Her grip on the broom handle tightened. "My family has lived here for three hundred years, Mrs. Wiggins. I have no intention of getting out of town."

"That's just an expression of incredulity. Sorry

about that. What does my mother wear to work?"

"Blue jeans." She spit the words out, like one might expel a bite of rotten fruit.

"So that explains why she got them! But how do you know the jeans are for work? And what makes you think it's remodeling? Have you been over there?"

Gladys Kravitz shuddered. "Gracious, no! But they're always dressed like workers, and sometimes they come in a van with stepladders and paint and such. Once they even had a truck deliver plywood and wallboard." The chin had been edging upwards, and she lowered it again to give me a penetrating look. "Mrs. Wiggins, what on earth is going on over there?"

"Beats me! Just wait until I get my hands on Mama."

The wail of an approaching siren must have drowned out some of my words. "You beat your mama?" Mrs. Kravtiz asked. Both chin and broom were held protectively in front of her as she backed up the steps.

Thank heavens the police had arrived.

The two blue-clothes officers were courteous and reasonably bright. But because I continue to live in this beautiful city, I will not use their real names. The female officer I'll call Cheech, and the male officer Chong.

"You said the wall was stolen, but it's right there."
Cheech was a plain woman with the no-nonsense air
of a high school librarian—well, at least the librarian
at my school. Miss Bernice Utternot had a stare that
could make incorrectly filed books line up on their
own, in complete accordance with the Dewey Deci-
mal System.

"I said tiles were stolen from the wall."

"The wall looks unmarked," Cheech said. She ran a
sturdy finger along the wall. "There is no evidence to
support the fact that there were tiles here."

"Well, there were tiles here. Dozens of them, in
fact."

Chong, who was by far the shortest officer I'd ever
seen, couldn't keep his eyes off me. In fact, they went
straight to my ring finger, where they registered a
flash of disappointment, but then moved slowly over
the rest of body. He seemed to like what he saw. Perhaps I was the first full-grown woman he'd ever met
that he actually towered over. Whatever it was, I had
the distinct feeling that I turned him on.

"Did you observe them being taken?" Chong
asked.

"No, sir."

"Were you alone when you discovered them
missing?"

"Yes, sir."

"Are you alone a lot, Mrs. Washburn?"

"Excuse me?"

Cheech cast her partner a Miss Utternot look. "Were there any other witnesses who saw the tiles on the wall?" she asked.

"Yes, ma'am. At least eleven people, including Sergeant Scrubb."

"Sergeant Scrubb the detective?"

"Yes, ma'am."

"When was this?"

"Two nights ago. When the incident happened."

"What incident was that?"

"When Madame Woo-Woo the psychic got poisoned. Everyone else got poisoned too—well, they only thought they had. Still, they insisted on going to MUSC and having their stomachs pumped. But then, you already know all about this, I'm sure."

Cheech nodded curtly. "That," she said wagging a finger, "was a waste of taxpayers' money."

"I don't think so," I ventured. "I'm pretty sure my mama will be getting a bill."

"It was still a misuse of resources. What if there had been a multiple vehicle accident on I-26? Those ambulances would have been needed."

"You've got a point, but just for the record, *I* was not one of the folks who used them."

"Well"—she gave Chong a look that was clearly an order—"we've got to get back to work."

"This is your work," I said, with the patience of a saint.

"There was nothing in Sunday's report about tiles."

She touched the wall one last time. "There's nothing here, Mrs. Washburn. There never was. Have you considered counseling?"

"I'm not crazy! And what about the footsteps I heard upstairs? You haven't even been up there yet."

Chong waved his arm like a schoolboy. "I'll go up there with Mrs. Washburn."

"I don't think so. Y'all have the guns, not me."

"Neither of us is going upstairs," Cheech barked. She turned her broad back on me and started out the kitchen door.

That's when I lost control. You have to believe me when I say I've never done anything remotely like this before. I don't know what possessed me to grab a copper tea kettle—half-filled with water—from C.J.'s stove and fling it at the freshly painted wall. But I did.

And that's when the peculiar odor filled the room.

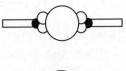

9

It smelled at first like a dead hamster. Just for the record, I haven't had a whole lot of experience smelling dead hamsters, although my son Charlie had a pet hamster named George that disappeared one fine day in May. When, after a thorough search, the little fellow wasn't found, we assumed he'd made his escape through the window since there was a hole in the screen. It wasn't until October, when we turned on the furnace for the first time that season, that we learned what really happened to George.

The odor emanating from C.J.'s punctured drywall smelled more like ten dead Georges. It was strong enough to make Cheech cover her nose and mouth with her hands. Chong, however, didn't seem to notice a thing.

"What the hell is that?" Cheech had turned around when the kettle hit the wall.

"Heck if I know." I grabbed a dishtowel from the

oven door handle and held it over my mouth. Even with the towel for a filter, my stomach did a couple of turns as I approached the hole—really a half-moon gash caused by the bottom of the kettle.

I closed one eye and peered inside. There wasn't much to see but darkness. My head, small as it is, kept blocking the light. I crouched and tried to look up. More of the same. I arched my back and looked down. Finally I saw something; a bit of white, a hint of blue.

"What do you see?" Cheech demanded.

"I'm not sure. I'm going to need a flashlight. Or else we need to make this hole bigger."

"I'll get it," Chong said.

I thought the little man was going to bring me the torch. Instead he elbowed me aside, and then in a remarkable display—given his slight build—he ripped off a huge chunk of the drywall with his bare hands.

"There," he said with a grin. "That was a man's job."

Cheech loomed over both of us. "Well? What the hell is in there?"

Chong and I vied for viewing space. Alas, being smaller and quicker, I won. That was my first mistake. My second mistake was to reach into the hole and touch what I saw. I still don't know why I did that, except that for the second time that morning, I was having trouble believing my eyes.

Again, I needn't have doubted them. That was definitely a skeleton, wedged between the kitchen and dining room walls. The part of the skull I touched—the forehead—was smooth and white. The cheeks, however, still had desiccated tissue clinging to them, and there appeared to be a full head of long brown hair. I couldn't really see the body because it was wrapped in a blue shawl, but I could tell— maybe it was the hair—that the deceased had been a woman.

I took a few steps backward, pushing my way past Cheech, and sat on the floor. It was Chong's turn to peek. He took only a few seconds, and then appeared to pass out.

This reaction didn't seem to surprise Cheech at all. She merely pulled her partner aside and peered into the hole, her ample derriere looking for all the world like a large globe in that position. While the woman took her sweet time staring at the remains, I contemplated the theory of continental drift. Finally Cheech turned and straightened.

"What do you know about this?"

"No more than you do, although I'd say it's a safe bet we just found C.J.'s ghost."

"Ghost?"

"Well, Apparition American would be a more sensitive way to put it. Anyway, this house is clearly haunted. Here's the reason why."

"Nonsense. Ghosts don't exist." Cheech didn't possess quite the upper body strength the diminutive Chong possessed, but with the aid of one of C.J.'s butcher knives, and a screwdriver I found in a drawer, she managed a fairly speedy demolition. Meanwhile, the prone Chong caught up on a few Zs.

I watched with horror and fascination as the fully clad figure of a woman was exposed. Somehow I'd missed that, atop all that brown hair, was a white drawstring cap. Beneath the shawl, and extending the length of her body, was a loose gown. She was barefoot.

"Nightclothes," I heard myself say.

"Maybe. That's for me to determine."

"Shouldn't we call the police—I mean, Sergeant Scrubb?"

Cheech gave me a look that could have withered a silk flower. Then she reached into the wall cavity and tried to extract the corpse.

"Stop that."

Cheech froze. "What did you say?"

"I said leave her alone."

"That's what I thought you said. May I remind you, Mrs. Washburn, that it was you who found me the knife and screwdriver."

"Yes, but it's one thing to get a better look, and quite another to actually disturb her. I mean, shouldn't we at least call a minister first?"

"Dead is dead," Cheech grunted, "and I sure the hell don't need you telling me how to do my job."

"I'm not telling—merely suggesting. It's just that it seems wrong."

"Then close your eyes. Better yet, wait in the next room." Cheech returned to her grizzly task.

"Leave her alone!" I'm physically incapable of roaring, but I can manage a loud squeak when properly motivated.

Cheech ignored me. Bones fell out of the loose gown. The skull tipped back and—well, I won't go into details. I felt both sick to my stomach and mad as hell. This was a real person whose sanctity was being violated.

I had no option but to sucker punch Cheech on her ample behind. I hit her square in the middle of South America, launching her forward into the hole. In retrospect, I only made matters worse.

Sergeant Scrubb shook his head. "Abby, I really wish you wouldn't have done that."

"But she was desecrating the corpse. Surely that wasn't the proper procedure."

We were in his office, where I'd been released in his custody. He sat behind a desk that looked like an exploded mail truck, and I perched on the edge of an ancient and institutional wood chair. He sighed as he leaned over the mess and handed me a tepid cup of coffee the consistency of molasses. I'd asked for milk and sugar, and had gotten artificial sweetener and a landslide of that powdered cream substitute.

"Believe me," the detective said, "those two will be reprimanded. I wouldn't be surprised if Cheech (he used her actual name) is suspended."

"And what will happen to me?"

"Essssss," he said, sucking in through his teeth.

"That bad, huh? Well, if Charleston City Jail is going to be home, do I at least have a choice of outfits? I mean, in case you haven't noticed, I'm a little on the short side for horizontal stripes."

He chuckled. "Abby, prisoners don't wear stripes anymore, at least not in city jails. But they do wear shackles—which reminds me, I need an ankle measurement."

I could feel the blood drain from my face, and since it didn't have far to go, the aforementioned ankles swelled. It occurred to me that this was a good thing. If I put my feet up later on, the swelling would go down and I might be able to slip out of the shackles.

"Abby, I was only kidding! You look like you've seen a ghost."

"No shackles?"

Scrubb shook his head and laughed. "I'm not even going to lock you up."

"You're *not?*"

"Nah. I'm just supposed to put the fear of God in you a bit. Punching a cop is a serious offense, but there weren't any witnesses now, were there?"

"You're right. It's just my word against hers. Officer Chong was still out cold."

He smiled. "Officer Chong is originally from up the road a piece. What can you expect?"

"You mean a Yankee?"

"Yeah, from one of the square states, I believe."

"Shame on us," I said. "My granddaddy was a Yankee."

"And so was my mama."

We hung our heads in mutual shame for a moment. Most folks can't help where they're born, and those who can—well, they must have had darn good reasons for choosing the northern tier.

Officer Scrubb broke our minute of silence. "As for Officer Cheech, she's a rookie—a transfer in from another part of South Carolina. She's not typical of the Charleston Police Department."

That was quite true. The Charleston Police Department, under the brilliant leadership of Chief Reuben Greenberg, is one of the finest in the country.

"Well," I said, as the dust from my sigh of relief settled, "I guess I'll just be skedaddling then." I set my coffee cup on the corner of his desk. The plastic spoon stood at a forty-five degree angle, not touching the rim.

Sergeant Scrubb stepped between me and the door. "Just one more thing, Abby."

"You can have my firstborn," I wailed. I meant that literally. Neither Sergeant Scrubb nor my daughter Susan was married. True, the sergeant had a good ten years on my daughter, but that just meant he was financially more secure. And quite possibly more mature.

Scrubb laughed again. "You can keep your firstborn—for now, at least. I'm already in a relationship. But I'll let you know if that falls through."

"She's real pretty," I said, to cement the thought. "She's a good six inches taller than me and blond—well, in the chemical sort of way. So, what's the one more thing?"

His demeanor became professional again. "First you have to promise me that you won't meddle in this case. No matter what."

"I promise."

"And what I'm about to say is confidential. Do you understand? You are not allowed to tell *anyone*."

"Not even Greg?"

"Greg you can tell. In fact, I plan to call him this evening. Professional courtesy, you might say."

Until we moved to Charleston, my husband Greg had been one of Charlotte, North Carolina's top detectives. In fact, some of his coworkers took to calling him Columbo, despite the fact that Greg is a good deal younger than Peter Falk and has never owned a trenchcoat.

Without being invited this second time, I took a seat. I have a fairly well developed intuition, and my inner voice was screaming at rock concert decibels.

"Sock it to me," I said.

Scrubb cleared his throat. "Your fingerprints were on the cassette recorder we retrieved from under Miss Cox's dining room table."

"I told you I tampered with the tape. It was just a joke, for crying out loud."

"Yes, and I can see the humor in it. Unfortunately, your fingerprints weren't the only thing the lab boys found."

He paused so long that rap musicians the world over grew old and died, their music along with them. "What did they find?" I practically shrieked.

"Poison."

"Poison? What kind?"

"That, I'm not at liberty to say."

"Which really means you don't know, right?"

Scrubb frowned. "Damn women's intuition. But the lab's working on it. At any rate, it was apparently absorbed through the skin. When she pressed the buttons."

I frowned as well. "Which means," I said, thinking aloud, "that the poison was applied to the buttons sometime between my arrival at the house and the when the séance began."

He nodded. "Abby, I'm not asking about your mother—so don't get me wrong. But is there any possibility that Miss Cox could have been involved?"

"Could have been involved? Is that a euphemism for cold-blooded killer?"

"You sound angry?"

"No, I don't. I sound mad as hell. C.J.—and I've made this clear in the past—is the type of woman who helps bugs get out of the garden fountain. After a rain once, I saw her pick worms off the sidewalk and put them back into the grass."

"Okay, I get the picture. In that case, how long was it between the initial guest's arrival, and the beginning of the séance?"

I cocked my head to think. "I'm not sure, because we served refreshments first. Madame Woo—what's-her-name—insisted on that. The later we started the séance, she claimed, the better. I think she just wanted to make sure she got to eat—in case the séance was a bust. Well, she was right on that score, wasn't she?"

"How long, Abby?" Sergeant Scrubb was a patient man, but he didn't suffer fools.

"I'd have to guess. Between forty-five minutes and an hour."

"And did the guests have access to the dining room where the séance was held?"

"Well, it wasn't shut off, or anything. But we didn't eat in there. We loaded up our plates and ate in the living room. The medium insisted on that too. She wanted to 'maintain the sanctity of the space'—whatever that means."

"Sounds like church talk. So, theoretically anyone could have had access to the table, and therefore the recorder."

"Right. And that includes Madame Woo-Woo."

"Are you suggesting she might have killed herself?"

I shrugged. "It wouldn't hurt to keep an eye on the bank accounts of her family and friends, would it? Assuming you can do such a thing."

"Why would I do that?"

"To see if any major insurance policies have been cashed in."

Scrubb used a stub of a pencil to jot down a few notes. I couldn't believe he hadn't thought of that on his own. Or perhaps he had, and he was playing me like a well-tuned fiddle. In any case, it wouldn't hurt to toss him a few more notes.

"The best time for one of the Hustlers to have tampered with the machine was while I was out on the front steps doing the greeting, or just after, when I helped Mama serve the cake."

The stub was worn to a nub by more scribbling. "You know, Abby, you just might have missed your calling."

I beamed with cautious pride, lest he was just fiddling with my fiddle. "Anytime you want to bounce ideas off me, you know where I live."

"I do. And that's where I hope to find you."

"I beg your pardon?"

"Abby, the last time you got involved in a case, you remember what happened?"

"Yes, but that was different! That person wanted me dead."

"You can't assume this person doesn't want the same thing. Abby, you are to stay completely out of this. Do you understand? I realize you have a shop to run, but you have an assistant now. If it isn't necessary to go in, I'd just as soon you didn't."

"So what does this mean? Are you putting me under house arrest?"

"Not yet." He gave me a faint smile. "But if I need to. . . . Let's hope for both our sakes, that I don't."

"That sounds like a threat," I growled. A small part of me will always be a teenager.

"Consider it advice. Incidentally, Greg called from the boat. He's having trouble getting back into port. Something to do with the tide."

There were footsteps outside the door and guarded voices. Familiar voices. Then a soft knock.

"Ah." Scrubb looked relieved. "Your escort has arrived."

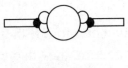

10

"My *what?*"
He opened the door. There stood my two second-best friends in the world—after C.J.—looking miserable and embarrassed.

The Rob-Bobs, as I call them, are life partners Rob Goldburg and Bob Steuben. Their shop, The Finer Things, was across the street from mine up in Charlotte; now it is literally next door. I think of the men as the brothers I wish I had. My own brother, Toy, heterosexual to a fault, is now in seminary training to be an Episcopal priest. But until this recent development, he had time for every other woman on the planet except for Mama and me. Years went by when he lived out in California, parking cars for the stars (being a star was his ambition), and we saw neither hide nor hair of him. He wasn't even willing to pick up the phone when we called.

But I digress. The Rob-Bobs are good friends—not double-crossers. Cross-dressers maybe—well, just

Bob, and only upon occasion. If they were in on some plot to limit my freedom, they had every right to look miserable and embarrassed.

"Well, well," I said, "if it isn't Judas II, and his buddy, Judas III."

"Abby!" Sergeant Scrubb said with surprising sharpness. "Be fair. They didn't volunteer for this assignment. We asked them to come."

"The 'we' being you and Judas IV stuck out on the boat?" When Greg did get in with his load of shrimp, *this* shrimp wasn't taking any of his load. Believe me, for the foreseeable future, the temperature in our boudoir was going to be on the frosty side.

"Abby, be reasonable." That was Rob Goldburg, a handsome man in his early fifties who looks like a younger James Brolin. Bob Steuben, by the way, makes a passable Barbara Streisand at costume parties, and he can even sing vaguely like her, although his normal speaking voice is a basso profundo.

"Reasonable?" I shrieked. "How would you feel about having baby-sitters?"

"We're not here to baby-sit you," Bob boomed. "We just want to show you a good time until Greg gets back."

"Don't you have a shop to run?"

"What's the point of having an assistant? Carmen can run it."

"Good for her. I still don't need a sitter."

Rob's grin could charm six legs off a spider. "Come on, Abby, we'll have a good time."

"Can we go shopping?" I don't mean to stereotype these two, or to imply that all gay men have great fashion sense, but these two are a blast to shop with. Whereas Greg sits outside the dressing room, slumbering, until I poke him to prompt an opinion, the Rob-Bobs bring armloads of clothes for me to try on. What's more, their taste jibes with mine.

"Absolutely. Where do you want to start?"

"Saks, here we come!"

"And then," Bob said, "I'm treating you to lunch."

"Where? At Magnolias, or Slightly North of Broad?"

"Abby," Rob said gently, "he wants to make it."

That put the kibosh on my quiche. Bob Steuben fancies himself a gourmet cook. Perhaps he is—if you go in for such things as Albino Eels en croute, or Marinated Emu Tenderloins on a Bed of Goat Cheese-Infused Potatoes.

"Well, instead of Saks downtown, why don't we shop at Dillards up at Northwoods Mall. We could grab a bite at the food court?"

Sergeant Scrubb cleared his throat. "Would you three mind making your plans outside? I have some paperwork to catch up on."

We stepped into the hall, and Rob pulled the door shut behind him. "We could do it all. Sort of like a scavenger hunt." He leaned down and whispered in my ear. "Bob's already got lunch planned; Fennel-Seared Pig Tails with Rhubarb Chutney and Essence of Pigeon Droppings."

"Hey, I heard that! Don't believe a word of it, Abby. I'm not telling you what it really is—it's a surprise. But here's a hint. When it was alive, it had three heads."

That did it. That's when I decided to be naughty and take advantage of my friends.

"Speaking of scavenger hunts," I said. "I just remembered I'm supposed to be on one." I glanced at my watch and gasped. "Right now!"

The men exchanged incredulous looks. "Abby, are you on the level?" Rob asked.

"Cross my heart and hope to die, stick a needle in my eye." I know, that's a horrible oath, and I was taking a chance, but we all have to go sometime, don't we? Just as long as that needle part didn't come true.

"Is this for some kind of club initiation?" Bob asked. "I've heard about all these secret Charleston societies, but I thought one's family had to live here for centuries before they even considered asking you to join."

"Something like that," I said. He was right about the societies—or so I've heard. At least that part wasn't a lie.

Rob whistled. "Wow, I'm impressed. What do you have to collect on the hunt?"

I've always prided myself on my ability to think fast on my feet, despite the fact that they are size four. This time I outdid myself.

"The first item is a photocopy of a pedigree—a very old pedigree. Let's see, then there's a crystal ball, a toy car, a thesaurus, a doggy chew toy, and a stock market tip."

"Abby, that sounds like fun. I don't suppose that we can play as well?"

"Officially no, but you can drive me from house to house."

I caught Bob preening in the reflection of a glass door as he passed. "Do we get to come inside?"

"I'm afraid not, but you can help me navigate. You see, the candidate who travels the least miles, and in the least length of time, gets extra points." I glanced at my watch again. "Oh, dear, I'm running out of time."

"Let us be off then," Rob said gaily. Whenever the dear man gets excited he affects a British accent, even though he's Carolina born and bred.

Off we went.

I remembered that chiseled cheeks Chiz had an up-stairs office on Meeting Street. I'd seen the discreet real estate sign any number of times, and thought to myself that if I ever needed to sell my home at number seven Squiggle Lane, I'd choose Chiz. It was my theory that a sign that small and classy meant there had to be an opulent office somewhere, paid for by a booming business.

The Rob-Bobs parked on Society Street and remained in their car, listening to classical music, while I trotted over to Meeting. If they feared that I would bolt, they gave no sign. It was wonderful having folks trust me so much, and yes, I felt guilty for betraying that trust. But it was for a good cause, was it not? Besides, the guys were having fun.

My instincts were right. Chisel Cheeks had an office that was better appointed than most homes I've seen. The dark paneling was mahogany, the lamps antique Tiffany, and the royal blue carpet so plush and soft, I lost an inch of height. *That*, I would have to change.

Chiz's secretary was also well-appointed, but not about to let me see her boss without an appointment. Her silicone bosoms bobbled as she shook her bleached blond head.

"This is an *exclusive* agency, Mrs. Washburn. We don't allow walk-ins."

"Tell him I flew."

"You don't understand, Mrs. Washburn. This is an *exclusive* establishment."

"Gotcha. This is an *excluuuuusive* place. Now, may I please see Mr. Banncock—or Chiz, as we like to call him."

A professionally plucked brow rose. "You're a friend of Mr. Banncock?"

"Well—"

I'd hesitated too long. "I'm afraid you'll have to make an appointment, Mrs.Washburn. Did you bring your credentials?"

"I beg your pardon?"

"Your *credentials*." She said it so slowly, exaggerating the syllables, that I was able to count every one of her capped teeth.

I graced her with a sweet smile. "I heard you the first time, ma'am. What credentials would that be?"

She threw her hands up in despair. The multicolored acrylic nails flashed like a Roman candle.

"Your lineage—your family tree."

"Excuse me?"

She tapped the desktop with those awful nails. "Were they here, in the Holy City, before the war?"

Charleston is fondly referred to as the Holy City because of its myriad church steeples. But I wasn't sure what she meant by the "war." Elsewhere in the South it would undoubtedly be the Civil War—or the War of Northern Aggression, depending on your point of view. Charleston is, however, much older and more genteel than most of the region.

"Do you mean the Late Unpleasantness, or the Colonial Rebellion?"

"That last one—the Revolutionary War. Do you have proof your family settled on the peninsula before then? Mr. Banncock handles only those clients who can prove their families resided in the Holy City before the war."

If brains were dynamite, I wouldn't have enough to blow my nose. I should have known all along that she was talking about bloodlines.

"Why, that's discrimination!" I cried.

She pretended to shuffle papers on her desk. Since she had only one paper, that was a pretty neat trick. I was tempted to ask her to clap with one hand.

"It's not discrimination," she said. "For your information, Mr. Banncock has lots of black customers. Plenty of African Americans were here before the war."

"Against their will! Besides, I know for a fact that not all of his clients come from old families."

That got her attention. "Like who?"

"Like my friend C.J. Jane Cox, her real name is. Chiz," I said, taking the opportunity to use his first name, "sold her a house."

Acrylic claws tapped on the computer keyboard for a few seconds. "Actually, you're wrong, Mrs. Washburn. It says right here that her great-great-great-great grandfather, Cornelius Willow-Worth Ledbetter was a tea merchant who built a house on Legare Street in 1708."

"Let me see that!" I remembered my manners. "Please."

"I'm afraid I've already said too much, Mrs. Washburn. Client information—"

"Did I mention that you have beautiful hair?"

The claws stroked the lacquered do. "Really?"

"Have you ever thought about acting?"

"Well, as a matter of fact, I was an extra in *The Patriot*. You know, that Mel Gibson movie they filmed here."

"Get out of town!" My enthusiasm was genuine. I would never cheat on my husband Greg, but if I did, it would be with Mel.

"Honest, I was."

"Did you get to meet Mel?"

"Nah. But one of the cameramen said I was real cute, and he'd be happy to take some pictures of me—you know, for my portfolio."

"And did he?"

"Nah. Made me sleep with him for nothing."

"Men are pigs." Not all men are pigs, of course. But I could speak from experience about one. Buford was the king of porkers—when he wasn't busy being a timber snake.

She paused, as if chewing gum, but there was nothing in her mouth, that I could see, except for those fabulous fakes. "Oh, what the hell." She printed what was on her computer screen, which comprised several printed pages, and handed it to me. "You said she was a friend—and this will give you an idea of what we're looking for. Besides, and I wasn't going to tell you this, Mr. Banncock isn't in today."

"Out showing houses?"

She shrugged her God-given shoulders, causing her manmade mammae to bobble again. "I don't know, and that's the truth. He's been really secretive these last couple of days. Not that he ever talks very much—and the phone . . . well, he might as well not even have one. I haven't gotten a call all day. Not that I'm complaining, mind you."

"So business is bad?"

"Oh no, we sell plenty of houses—just not as many as other real estate agents I've worked for, on account of our—uh—"

"Exclusivity?"

"Yes, ma'am. But don't get me wrong, Mr. B makes a bundle off the ones he sells."

I looked around at my plush surroundings. "I'm sure he does. You said that Chiz had been secretive the last couple of days. Do you mean since the séance?"

"How did you know?"

"Because I really do know Chiz. I was at the séance too, you see." I sighed. "I was hoping he could give me the address of a couple that was there. I seemed to have lost it."

"What are their names?"

"Riffle. Hugh and Sondra."

This time the clacking was music to my ears. "Yeah, here they are. Say, isn't he the one who does those car commercials? You know, with the dead celebrities' cars?"

"That's him. Gross, isn't it?"

"Not really. I was thinking how cool it would be to

buy one of those cars, because not everyone would have one, you know. Do you think he has any late model Porsches?"

"Possibly." For all I knew, he did.

The keys clacked one last time. "Here. That's their home address." She stood. "Promise not to tell?"

"Cross my heart and hope to—cross it again."

"I'm off to buy me a brand-new car—well, a brand-new used car. Mr. Banncock can answer his own damn phone."

"Did you get it?" They'd switched from classical to oldies and I could barely distinguish Bob's bass from one of the Righteous Brothers.

I turned off the radio and waved the papers the lonely receptionist had given me. "And you wouldn't believe whose pedigree this is."

"Babs?" Bob boomed.

"Guess again. It's our very own C.J."

Rob snatched the Ledbetter family tree from my hot little hand. He scanned it, mumbling to himself. Finally he passed it back to Bob, who was sitting in the rear seat.

"That's impressive."

"If you can believe it," I sniffed. "All she ever talks about is Shelby. I wouldn't be surprised if she made up that pedigree, just like she makes up everything else."

Bob reached forward and patted my shoulder.

"Now, now, Abby, let's not be too hard on her. Some of the stories we thought she made up have actually turned out to be true."

"Name one!"

"Well—like the time she bet us she could lick her ears with her tongue."

Rob laughed. "That was something! I still think she should make it into the *Guiness Book of World Records* for that."

"Harrumph," I said, borrowing from Ella Nolte. "And it doesn't prove that she's part giraffe. Those little bumps you can feel on her head are *not* horns."

Rob winked. "Sounds like our Abby is a bit jealous."

"I am not! Who needs a stupid pedigree anyway? So what if I never get invited to join Charleston's inner circle? I still have loser friends that can't get in either. I have you two."

"Touché!" Bob boomed.

"More like touchy," Rob said, but he winked again. "Okay, how about we get this show on the road. What's next? The crystal ball?"

"Toy car," I mumbled.

"I'd swear you said it was going to be a crystal ball. Didn't she, Bob?"

"That she did."

"Well, I was mistaken."

The truth is, I'd decided to pay my visit to Sondra Riffle at home, rather than Hugh at his place of business. She seemed less intimidating. The only problem was that I knew Hugh gave away toy cars to every customer that visited his grisly lot, but I doubted if Sondra dispensed them to uninvited visitors. If she didn't, I was going to have to find a way to buy one.

Staying ahead of the Rob-Bobs was going to be a challenge.

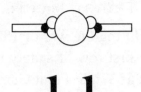

11

The Riffles lived in a magnificent Greek Revival mansion right on East Battery, arguably the city's most desirable location. The couple were not natives, hailing originally from Louisiana, and were part of the influx of latter settlers that has raised real estate values throughout the peninsula. Their house, if I remembered correctly—I comb the real state transaction page religiously—was sold to them for 7.2 million dollars. Chiz Banncock was not their agent, by the way, seeing as how they lacked the proper plasma. But the very fact that they were in his electronic address book was proof that there was a degree of exclusivity that could be purchased.

The High Battery is a sea wall that protects the southeast corner of Charleston from hurricane tides. It is here that the Ashley River and the Cooper River come together to form the Atlantic Ocean. The wall derives its name from the battery of guns that defended the city during the war of 1812. Between the sea wall and the first row of stately homes is a park, officially known as White Point Gardens. At the east end is a marker commemorating the hanging of the so-called "gentleman pirate," Stede Bonnet in 1718. The Holy City was suffering from a rather pesky pirate problem, and by the end of the year a total of forty-nine pirates were hanged at that location and buried nearby. Stede Bonnet was perhaps the most interesting of the lot because he was a man of letters, and owned a profitable sugar plantation on the island of Barbados.

The Battery, as White Point Gardens is commonly called, is today a pleasant park graced by sweeping live oaks, and spectacular views of the Atlantic's birthing. It would be a peaceful place to stroll were it not for the hordes of tourists that descend on it each summer, despite the wilting heat. In addition to the buses, cars, and foot traffic, there are horse-drawn carriages. The last, although charming, lend a redolence to the air that can, at times, assault one's olfactory senses. Sure, the horses wear nappies, but they don't always hit the mark, if you know what I mean.

We found a place to park on East Battery Street opposite the harbor, and a popular stop for tour buses. When I got out of Rob's car a group of happy Japanese were taking pictures of other members of their party taking pictures of far-off Fort Sumter. I volunteered to take a picture of the ones photographing picturetakers, thus making everyone all that much happier. It always warms my heart to do a good deed, and I was in an upbeat mood when I rang the Riffles' doorbell. The Rob-Bobs, by the way, had elected to sit on a bench in the park and critique tourists.

The Riffle mansion had a double staircase leading to the front door. Some tour guides would have you believe that the stair on the left was for gentlemen, the one on the right for ladies, lest the former glimpse the latter's ankles. Architectural historians will tell you that this is nonsense; the two stairs provide balance. Just to be contrary, I took the gentlemen's stair.

I fully expected that a liveried butler—or at least a maid—would answer the door. I was surprised to see Sondra standing there. Perhaps she had been expecting a UPS delivery, because she seemed surprised as well.

"Oh," we said simultaneously, "it's you."

"Jinx, you owe me a coke," I said.

"I beg your pardon?"

"Nothing—it's just a silly saying. I know it's terribly rude of me to just drop in like this, but I really need to speak to you. Do you have a minute?"

Although it was almost noon, she was dressed in

pink silk pajamas and had a bad case of bed hair. Curiously, she seemed torn by my question.

"Of course," she finally said, and ushered me through a hall lined with black marble statues on white pedestals and into a grand salon. I'd expected tacky from a couple who sold dead celebrity's cars, but boy howdy, was I wrong. The grand room was done in green; not the so-called burnt shades so popular in the nineties, or the ubiquitous hunter, but a refreshing mint. The furniture was predominantly French, although besides the slew of Louies, there was a small walnut William and Mary bureau with a herringbone border. It was the sort of piece that would have given the twins on *Antique Roadshow* spasms of joy, had they seen it when they were in town. Clearly, Sondra had been one of the thousands unable to get a ticket to that event.

She saw me eyeing the piece. Fortunately, I had my mouth shut, so I was not drooling on the Aubusson carpet.

"That piece came with the house," she said. "Can you believe that?"

I shook my head. "It's exquisite. Have you had it appraised?"

"I don't intend to sell it. Actually"—she bit her tongue before continuing—"Hugh won't let me sell it."

"I had a husband like that once—a real control freak."

"Mr. Washburn?"

"Gracious, no! Greg's a sweetheart. My first husband, Buford—I just remembered he's in town right now—dumped me when I got too old for him. Traded me in for a bimbo with silicone parts—" My mouth snapped shut like a frog on a fly. I couldn't believe I'd mentioned silicone to a woman with more plastic parts than Barbie.

Again, Sondra was on to me. "I know what you're thinking, and you're absolutely right. I have had plastic surgery. Tons of it, in fact."

"You have?" It was the only polite response.

She nodded. "Care for a drink?"

That explained the pajamas and rumpled look so late in the day. I seldom drink—finding the aftereffects unpleasant, not to mention fattening—and almost never before five.

"Have any tea?" In South Carolina, that word, without an modifiers, refers to what y'all north of the Line call iced tea. Unless otherwise specified, it is served sweetened—sometimes too sweet for Yankee tastes, which is odd, when you consider they put sugar in their cornbread and we don't.

At any rate, Sondra wrinkled her modified nose. "I believe there is a pitcher in one of the fridges—Hugh likes that stuff."

While she padded off in her bare feet to fetch me a glass of the noxiously innocuous beverage, I admired my surroundings. I couldn't have put together a better room—even with the Rob-Bobs' help. Of course my room would have a different life-size painting above the mantle. However, the portrait of Sondra, showing her seated from the waist up, was expertly done. She looked to be about twenty, her face glowing with youth and newfound wealth.

"Pretty, wasn't I?" she asked, appearing suddenly. She handed me a glass dripping condensation. Apparently she'd forgotten a napkin.

"Beautiful! You look so happy."

"I *was*." She motioned for me to sit, so I chose a Louis XV fauteuil chair with upholstered seat and back and carved legs. The fabric background was cream with pale pink roses on vinelike stems. If I spilled the sugary tea, I might stick to the chair, and thus would have a good excuse for taking it home with me. "And then," she said, picking up the thread of conversation again, "along about my fortieth birthday, everything went south—no offense, you understand."

"No offense taken."

"So, as you've already noticed, I tried doing something. Fat lot of good it did." Despite her soft, cultured voice, she had a grating laugh, not unlike an electric pencil sharpener.

"You certainly have a beautiful home," I said, desperate to change the subject. "Who is your decorator?"

"Me."

"You?"

The pencil got shorter. "Yes, I was a beauty queen—Miss Kudzu, Miss Regional Okra, and first runner-up in the Miss Hell Swamp contest, but I'm not stupid." She took a sip of something a lot stiffer than sweet tea. "I started out as a zoology major in college, because I love animals. But I switched to art history my first semester when they made us dissect frogs. Anyway, art history is not a very marketable education, so I got a job as an interior decorator. That's how I met Hugh. I decorated his first house. He was really into dark wood paneling and Italian leather sofas."

I smiled. Buford was pretentious enough to want antique furnishings, but Greg, bless his shrimp-catching heart, would love wood paneling and leather sofas. Throw in a large-screen TV, and he'd think it was heaven.

"How long have you two been married?" I asked.

"Twenty-eight years."

"Wow, that's a long time. I mean, that's longer than Buford and I were married."

She took a swig of comfort. "Want to know a secret?"

"Well—"

"He made me sign a pre-nup."

"Get out of town!" Buford didn't make me sign a prenuptial agreement, but he might as well have. He was a lawyer, and one of the good old boys. Need I say more?

Sondra managed a rueful smile. "I didn't know anything about money then. I'd always been poor. Miss Regional Okra doesn't pay anything—well, except for a year's supply of gumbo. I put myself through college on scholarships—*academic* scholarships. When I met Hugh I fell head over heels in love. He could have asked for my right arm, and I'd given him my left arm as well." She took a long drink of liquid courage. "Now, I'm afraid he doesn't want any part of me."

Having walked that road, I knew there was nothing I could say to make her feel better—not in the long term. It is, however, always a comfort to have one's feelings validated, and I could have bet on what she was feeling.

"Maybe we could get the diaper bag from one of those carriage horses and stash it in your husband's most expensive car."

She stared at me, not comprehending at first. When she did, her face lit up like a jack-o-lantern with two candles in it.

"We'd dump the contents out of the bag," she said, before giving that pencil a good sharpening.

"Of course. And we'd rub it into the seats."

We had ourselves a good laugh. We were on the verge of bonding—and why not, given the similarity of our unscrupulous husbands—when I remembered I was a woman with a mission.

"Tell me," I said, perhaps a bit too abruptly, "is there anyone in that little group of yours—the Heavenly Harlots—who might have had it in for Madame Woo-Woo?"

"That's Heavenly Hustlers," she said, still laughing. Her face grew serious. "You're not joking, are you?"

"Well, it wasn't me—so it had to be one of you."

"It could have been our hostess. Just between me and you, Abby—may I call you that?"

"By all means."

"Call me Sondra. As I was about to say, I'm not sure her elevator stops at all the floors."

I get very defensive when anyone, other than myself, or folks I know to be C.J.'s closest friends, comment on her mental condition. Her elevator *does* stop at all floors, including the penthouse. It's just that there are a few unscheduled stops as well.

"Jane Cox is a brilliant woman. She's minding my shop right now, singlehandedly."

Apparently Sondra couldn't decide whether to drink, laugh, or speak. She did a messy combination of all three.

"Damn," she said, referring to the stains on the

Aubusson, and then returned her attention to me. "If Miss Cox is as bright as you say she is, then why is she totally clueless to the fact that we've been fixing up her house for the last three weeks."

"Excuse me?" I'd been praying, in my lapsed Episcopalian sort of way, that Gladys Kravitz had been full of baloney. Given that her address was north of Broad, it would be a second-rate brand, of course.

"We—the Heavenly *Hustlers*—have been hustling our bustles off renovating that house."

"You're kidding," I said lamely.

"I wish I was. I have splinters and blisters to prove it." There were no end tables handy, so she held her drink between her knees and held up both hands. "I even broke a nail."

I shook my head. Mama's antics never cease to amaze me, and I'd bet my bottom dollar she was behind this. When she ran off to become a nun, she was actually accepted into an Episcopal convent, only to be expelled shortly thereafter for wearing curlers under her wimple, and singing on the stairs. The following year she became a torch singer in a seedy motel lounge, and was fired for singing altogether. She has tried to become a contestant on all the *Survivor* shows thus far; this last time receiving a letter from Jeff Probst begging her not to submit any more audition tapes. Apparently one of the producers had gotten a hernia from laughing too hard at one of her submissions.

"Why are y'all remodeling C.J.'s house, and whose idea was it?"

"It was your mother's idea—"

"I knew it!" Pretending to be surprised exonerated me from any culpability.

"We have a yearly project, you see. Mozella thought it would be fun—'a learning experience' is how she put it. I told her I'd had plenty of experience remodeling, and that even just from the customer's point of view, it could be a royal pain. And I was right. I tell you, Abby, your mother is a taskmistress to be reckoned with."

"Tell me about it. When I helped her shell peas as a kid, she had me sort them according to size and depth of color."

"Doesn't surprise me. But anyway, you get my original point about Miss Cox, don't you? A normal person would think it strange to find a wall replaced, or to have new ceiling fans magically appear."

"Did you say *wall*?"

"In a third floor bathroom. Water had gotten behind the wallboard, so we had to rip the whole thing out. Jeez, what a mess."

"Oh. Y'all didn't touch the kitchen wall?"

"The one with all the tiles?"

I nodded.

"No. Like I said, your mother kept us to a tight schedule. She wanted to make us start in the attic and work our way down, but we rebelled. It's just too hot for attics now. She settled for the third floor."

"And you all pitched in? Even your husband? I mean, I thought he was busy selling cars."

"Hugh helps out now and then. He's sort of a peripheral member of our group. He's got his work—so he's not as lonely as the rest of us. But Abby, you still haven't answered my question. Why hasn't she noticed?"

"She has, actually. She thinks it's a ghost."

Sondra rolled her eyes in a gesture worthy of any teenager. "Give me a break."

"You don't believe they exist?"

"Officially, or un?"

"Both."

"Well, officially I have to go along with that nonsense—Hugh's business depends on it, and that whole urban legend thing. But I've never seen a ghost, Abby. Have you?"

"I haven't actually seen one—but I've heard one."

This time, the eyes that had once gazed lovingly on the Miss Regional Okra tiara rolled so far back into her head they looked like Ping-Pong balls. "I'm afraid I'd need scientific proof."

It was pointless to argue. Besides, I'd strayed far from my mission.

"The night Madame Woo-Woo died," I said, "did you happen to notice anyone alone in the dining room? Between your arrival, of course, and the start of the séance?"

"Ella Nolte," she said without a second's hesitation. She drained the froth from the bottom of her glass of fortitude. "And don't unnecessarily read anything into that. Ella is a mystery writer, after all. She's supposed to be curious. She was probably just in there doing the same thing you did."

If she could roll her eyes, then it was perfectly all right for me to open mine wide in mock surprise. "What would that be?"

"Abby, we all know it was you who planted that recorder there."

"But it was just a joke."

"It's possible Ella had a joke or two of her own up her sleeve. You might want to ask her."

I hopped to my feet, and then realized, with a rush of joy, that my caffeine in the tea had gone straight through me—not literally, of course. But I always enjoy checking out folks' powder rooms. Especially the powder rooms of the very rich. The composition of bathroom fixtures can say a lot about someone. Solid gold, in my opinion, means the owner isn't really concerned about world hunger, or finding a cure for all forms of cancer. On the other hand, gold paint in a multimillion-dollar house means the owner may be putting on a show, and could be well on the way to bankruptcy. Gold plate, or a good-quality base metal, represent a balanced approach to life.

At any rate, while I am perfectly willing to ask to use the bathroom when I don't need to go, it always feels better if there is a genuine need. I raised my hand like a schoolgirl.

"May I use your bathroom before I go to see Ella?"

Sondra looked as if I'd asked something extremely personal—like her age. Or maybe her shoe size.

"Uh, I'm not sure it's very tidy. Heather—that's my housekeeper—has been off all week. Her mother up in Monck's Corner is sick."

"I promise not to look at anything—well, beyond what's necessary."

She led me to the room, which was much farther back in the house than I had expected. It delighted my soul to see that her good taste wasn't limited to the front rooms. Outside the bathroom door she stopped and laid a manicured hand on my shoulder. We were standing close enough so that I could smell the booze on her breath.

"The truth is," she said, "that Hugh spends a lot of time in this room."

"No problemo. I'll hold my nose."

I stepped inside and turned on the light. For a few seconds I thought I was hallucinating.

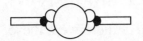

12

"And then what?" Rob asked. The men had been waiting patiently for my return, thanks to the Musical Muscle Boys, a men's glee club from San Francisco. The group was taking a self-guided walking tour of the city, and stopped to ask the Rob-Bobs directions. I'm sure my friends were able to give the visitors a couple of good pointers.

"You're not going to believe this, guys. Everything in that bathroom was cars."

"Cars?" Bob boomed.

"*Cars*. It was actually more than a powder room. It was a full bath—a very big bath. The tub was the inside of a little roadster. There was a little seat, and the spigot handle was a steering wheel. The outside had chrome bumpers. The toilet was hooked up to one of those machines you see in arcades, where you can test your driving skills. The sink was the inside of a very deep hubcap. Oh, and there was even a car-shaped terrarium on the vanity, with icky live things in it. And of course there were these." I pulled a small hand towel out of my blouse.

"Abby, you didn't!" they cried in unison.

"Jinx, you owe each other Cokes."

"You stole a towel?" Rob asked, his voice tinged with admiration.

"Borrowed. I fully intend to return it."

"But why? And Abby, isn't that stealing?" Bob, who hailed originally from Toledo, has solid Midwestern values. Which is not to say that we native-born Southerners don't have morals. It's just that we—oh heck, I was wrong, and I couldn't defend it. The best I could do was try and explain my actions.

"Because it has cars embroidered along the border," I said.

"Yes, but the rules call for a *toy* car?"

"Who says toys have to be three-dimensional?" I waved the towel. "Vroom, vroom."

"You're sick, Abby," Rob said, but he winked. "Oh, and speaking of sick, you'll never guess who we saw during our interminable wait."

"Besides the singing studs?"

"Only two were studs; the rest were duds. But yes, besides them."

"I give up, who?"

"I'll give you a hint." Rob held up his hand, which was made into a fist, save for his index and middle fingers, which were uncurled halfway. He shook his hand. "Hisssssss."

"Buford Timber Snake."

"You don't seem surprised."

"No. He came into the shop the day of the séance—oh my God! I stood him up!"

"Serves him right," Bob said. The Rob-Bobs are extremely protective of me. They are indeed the brothers my flesh and blood brother, Toy, should have been.

"But you don't understand. He seems to have changed. The very fact that he didn't make a fuss when I stood him up—well, that's not the Buford we all knew and hated, is it?"

"Got a point there."

"Well?" I demanded. "What did he say? Did he ask about me?"

Rob stood and laid a comforting arm around my shoulder. "We didn't speak to him. We saw him ride by in one of those horsedrawn carriages. We waved, and he waved back. That was it."

"I feel awful."

Bob was on his feet now, his arm around my other shoulder. I'm sure that to folks passing by, it looked like we were having a group hug. Or, if they couldn't see little ole me, they might have gotten the impression that the South was a lot more liberal than is normally believed to be the case.

"You could call him at the hotel," he said helpfully.

"No, I can't. I didn't even ask him where he was staying. Guys, I'm a self-absorbed witch, aren't I?"

They didn't argue.

"Guys!"

Rob squeezed the shoulder he'd appropriated. "No, you're not. But there's nothing you can do about it now. You can't very well be expected to call every hotel and motel in Charleston, now can you?"

"Buford would only stay at the best."

"Yes, but doesn't he have a history of staying in hotels under assumed names?"

"What?"

"You know," Bob practically bellowed, "like when he was cheating on you with Tweetie—oops!"

I shrugged their arms away. "I could call his Charlotte numbers. He was always compulsive about checking his voice mail."

"Sounds like a plan," Rob said. For a non-thespian, he was able to conjure up a remarkable amount of false enthusiasm. "But do it when we break for lunch. I figure we have just enough time for one more quest before then. What's next, Abby, the thesaurus, right?"

"Right!"

"But we still haven't collected the crystal ball!" Grown men with bass voices should refrain from whining.

"We'll get to the ball, dear," I said and gave Bob a smile full of sugar. "But the thesaurus is next."

It was almost scary how well my plan was working.

Ella Nolte was obviously a successful mystery writer. She lived only a few blocks away on Tradd

Street, in a pre-Revolutionary War house. The street got its name from Robert Tradd, thought to be the first child of English descent born there. The houses front right up to the sidewalk, giving it a European feel, and today it is still a highly desirable address. The Rob-Bobs, who had never been in a Tradd Street home, were dying to come inside with me.

"We could pretend that I'm your husband," Rob said. I'd never heard him sound so desperate.

Bob pushed his partner gently aside. "What about me?"

"Relax, guys. Neither of you gets the honor. She's already met Greg."

"When?" they chimed together. Coca Cola was going to make out like a bandit.

I couldn't very well tell them the truth now, could I? If they learned that Greg had met Thelma the night of Madame Woo-Woo's murder, they'd realize I was working on the case. I had to think creatively.

"You see," I said, "we were thoroughly prescreened for this test. We had to meet all the club members."

Rob's blue eyes narrowed as he gave the matter some thought. "Let me get this straight," he said, without a hint of irony, "you knew the people at the last stop?"

"Of course."

"And a towel was the best they could do?"

Bob scratched his head, which is beginning to lose its hair. He does it with some frequency, which answers for me the question of which came first, the chicken or the egg.

"Abby, what is the name of this secret society?"

"It's a secret."

"But we're two of your best friends."

"We're also your transportation," Rob said. "Not to mention, your guardians until Greg gets home."

"Okay, okay—uh, they call themselves the Tradd Street Irregulars."

"But they don't all live on Tradd."

"Which is why they're called irregulars."

Not only could Rob smell that something was rotten in Denmark, he could smell Copenhagen's city dump. "The rules of this scavenger hunt seem to be a tad flexible. What exactly are they?"

"Well, uh—I have to do my best to collect the items I mentioned, and like I said, I have to do it before six o'clock. And if I can't come up with exactly what's on the list, then I get the next best thing. *And,*" I said, for Bob's benefit, "I don't *have* to get everything on the list in order. It's just that I get extra points if I do."

The men exchanged glances. They'd been a couple for years, and are better at wordless communication than Greg and I.

"Well," Rob said finally, "we're going to take a little walk down to East Bay. We'll be back in about twenty minutes. Then *we're* going to eat."

"Gotcha."

I waited until they were out of earshot before ringing Ella Nolte's doorbell. I had to ring it three times before I got a response. Unfortunately I did nothing for the famous author's memory bell.

"You're the second tourist to bother me this morning," she said, in tones no native Charlestonian would ever have used. "The answer is 'no.' You may *not* see the inside of my house."

"I'm not a tourist," I wailed. "I'm Abigail Washburn. We met at Jane Cox's house. I was in the hoop skirt, remember?"

She peered down the length of her nose. It was a wonder she could see that far.

"Ah, yes. You operate a little thrift shop on King Street."

"It's not a thrift shop! I sell high-end antiques."

"Well, whatever." She just stood there, waiting for me to make the next move.

"I was wondering if you might autograph a book for me."

The nose, followed by the eyes, focused first on my pocketbook, which was barely large enough to hold a paperback, and then on my empty hands. She snorted.

"I don't see a book."

I tried to look surprised. "Drat! I must have forgotten the darn thing. I don't suppose you have one I could buy?"

"Harrumph."

"Is that a yes?"

"Mrs. Washburn, I do not sell my own books. I'm not *that* kind of a writer."

"What kind would that be?"

"Self-published."

"That's not such a good thing to be, eh?"

"I suppose that depends on how one likes one's books. I mean—and this is carrying the analogy a bit far, I admit—if you were in need of brain surgery, would you agree to have it performed by a physician who was self-taught?"

"No, of course not."

"And if you were emotionally disturbed, who would you prefer to discuss your problems with, a licensed professional, or your mother?"

"Mama."

"Harrumph."

Clearly, I'd given her the wrong answer. But it was the right one for me. I know for a fact—I've been keeping track—that Mama and I disagree on eighty percent of the things we discuss. In the days following our heart-to-hearts, I change my mind on thirty percent of the issues. On the other hand, I didn't agree with anything said by the two psychologists I went to when Buford dumped me. Never mind that Buford was the one who supplied them.

"I get the picture," I said. "You write quality books that have been properly edited. Are they humorous cozies? Do they contain recipes?"

She shuddered. "I write more serious fiction."

"I thought you wrote mysteries."

"They are novels of suspense—practically literary works, if I say so myself. My newest release, *Jabber Whacky*, is about a psychotic who talks himself out of a hospital for the criminally insane. It contains more themes than an English instructor's briefcase." She chuckled at her own joke.

"Get out of town! I read *Jabber Whacky!*"

She centered her probing proboscis on mine, and drilled me with her gaze. "Did you like it?"

"Loved it!" It was the truth, so help me. The critics, however, had hated it. One had called it "the worst piece of junk since the advent of the computer age. One hopes her PC threw up all over her." There was even an article in a national magazine—*People*, I think—about how the publisher had overestimated sales, resulting in a record number of returns. As a consequence the author had been dropped. This had, if memory served me right, happened some years ago. In the interim I'd forgotten the author's name. The catchy title was another matter.

Ella Nolte smiled for the first time since I'd met

her. "I think you should come inside. It's getting a little warm out here."

It was downright cold inside. Ella Nolte confessed that she'd been suffering from hot flashes lately, despite the fact that she believed she had completed "the change" several years ago.

"I think I'll talk to my doctor about hormone replacement therapy. Have you tried it?"

I was taken aback. I'm in my mid—okay, make it late, forties, but by all accounts, look young for my age. It is conceivable that I might have entered a precocious menopause, but certainly not something to be taken for granted. And Ella seemed to think of us as contemporaries.

"No, I haven't tried it. But I'll certainly look into it when I get to be your age."

"Harrumph."

"I'm forty-eight," I said.

"Mozella said she had you when she was fifteen. I happened to see your mother's driver's license and discovered she's seventy-eight."

"Which would make me sixty-three?" I would have stormed out of there, but still had lots of questions to ask. Mama, you can bet, was going to get a few questions as well.

"There's nothing wrong with sixty-three," Ella said. She gestured at her walls. "Look there. There's sixty-three of them."

She was referring to the enlarged book covers that hung on her walls in lieu of artwork. They all bore her name, but with the exception of *Jabber Whacky*, none of the titles was familiar. A few didn't even seem like mysteries. Judging by the cover of *Night of the Living Dreadlocks*, the author had once written horror novels.

"You've certainly been prolific," I said.

She smiled again. "Please, have a seat."

A large bookcase filled one wall, but there were only two seats to choose from. Both were, however, English wingbacks, dating to the 1770s, and appeared to have original needlepoint upholstery. I glanced around surreptitiously; at least that was my intent.

"Most of my stuff is in storage," she said, reading my mind.

"Well, these two chairs are very lovely." I hoisted myself into the one nearest me.

"I'd offer you tea," she said, "but I'm not originally from the South. I'm from Hackensack, New Jersey. So how about a glass of wine?"

"Wine would be divine." As long as I kept my consumption under half a glass, I'd be fine. I'm a cheap drunk.

She trotted off to the kitchen and returned in less than a minute with a glass of white wine. There was a trace of lipstick on the glass rim that matched the author's shade. She had poured a tumbler of water for herself.

"So, Mrs. Washburn," she said. "What is your agenda?"

"I beg your pardon?"

"What is your real reason for visiting me? Is it because I'm famous?"

I nodded.

"I figured that. It happens with some frequency, you know."

I nodded again. "I guess I have this thing for famous people. I saw the back of Johnny Bench's head in an airport once. I tell you, it made my day." I took a sip of wine, taking care to stay clear of the lipstick. "But there's something I wanted to ask you as well."

"Oh?"

"The night of the séance, between the time you arrived, and the beginning of the séance, did you see anyone alone in the dining room?"

She set the tumbler of water down on an Indian marquetry table. It was the only other piece of furniture in the room.

"Aha! You're trying to solve Madame Woo-Woo's murder, aren't you?"

"Guilty—not of the murder, I mean, but of trying to solve it."

"And so am I."

"You *are*?"

"Mrs. Washburn, you seem to have forgotten that I am a mystery writer. 'What ifs' are my stock in trade."

"So they are," I agreed, but rolled my eyes slightly in the direction of the *Night of the Living Dreadlocks* cover.

"I'll choose to ignore that," she said, proving that she was, at the least, a keen observer. "And the answer to your question is 'yes.' I did see someone in the dining room that evening, just fifteen minutes before the séance began."

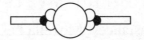

13

"Who was it?" I demanded.

The nose centered on my forehead, like the barrel of a gun. Her eyes, I decided, were the color of gunpowder. I would duck if I heard the click of a safety turned to off.

"Mozella Wiggins," she said, savoring each syllable. "Your mother, I believe."

"Yes, but that means nothing. Mama was cohosting the event, along with C.J. and I. She was probably just checking the table for dust. There's no crime in that."

"She was bent over looking under it. I could see her blue jeans."

"Yes, well, jeans under a hoop skirt is a crime. But surely you don't think she's capable of murder?"

"And you think one of the rest of us is?"

"Touché. But not Mama."

"Mrs. Washburn, we are all capable of the most heinous crimes, given the right motivation, and under the right circumstances. Mozella has shared with our little group some of her more imaginative exploits. She's not exactly the stereotype of your perfect little grandma."

"I'm well aware of her shenanigans. Murder is not among them."

"But she lies."

"Excuse me?"

"She said she gave birth to you when she was fifteen."

"She exaggerates to make a point. Isn't that what you do in your work?"

"I tell my lies to the blank page. There's a difference, you know."

I'd heard enough. "Ms. Nolte, you wouldn't happen to have a thesaurus I could borrow, would you? I promise to take very good care of it."

"I don't own a thesaurus."

"But you're a writer."

"Yes, and a good one. I have an extensive vocabulary, and I use it. If I needed to look up words all the time, I'd have no business being a writer."

I sighed and slid to my feet. The mission had to be scrubbed on two counts. To make matters worse, I'd forgotten myself and drunk from the smudged side of the glass.

"Harrumph."

"Huh? Never mind, I'll show myself out."

"I was about to say that I killed a thesaurus once."

"I beg your pardon?" Perhaps that hadn't been water in that tumbler, but vodka.

"In my very first mystery. *Who Killed Tyrannical Thesaurus Rex?* It didn't sell very well—that was the art department's fault, not mine—and a bunch were remaindered. I bought a carton of them, and still have a few in the back. Would you like one?"

"Yes, please."

While she strode off to fetch the book, I searched for its poster on the walls. There was none.

She was back in a flash. "Here," she said, and handed me a paperback with the worst cover art I'd ever seen. The dinosaur looked like Barney, only green, and he was holding a book under one arm. Both title and author's name looked like they'd been drawn in crayons, using as many colors as possible.

"It's an adult mystery," she said reading my mind again. "Some idiot made it look like a children's book."

"Wow. I feel for you." I waved the book. "Thanks, I really appreciate this."

"Seven-ninety-nine, please."

"What?"

"For the book. Like I said, I had to buy them myself."

"But the cover price is two bucks lower."

"Inflation. Do you want the book, or not?"

I gave her the ten, and when she said she didn't

have change, I told her to keep the extra money. I did, however, demand, and receive, an autograph. One of my choosing.

"To my very best friend, Abigail," it read, "who encouraged me in all my darkest hours."

"Did you get it?" the Rob-Bobs demanded in unison.

I showed them the paperback, but only the cover. We were standing on the sidewalk in front of Ella Nolte's house. The men had just returned from their walk, and had opened the car doors to allow the interior to cool.

Rob's patrician nose wrinkled when he saw the book. "I read that—or I tried to. Took it to the beach one year—a long time ago. Can't even remember when. But it was the worst book I'd ever read, and ever hope to read. Catchy title, Abby, and I love the artwork, but it doesn't count as a thesaurus."

"Of course it does. The word is right there on the cover. The rules don't say anything about it having to be an actual thesaurus."

Bob cleared his throat, sounding for all the world like a male bullfrog in mating season. "But it's implied, Abby."

"Look guys, y'all don't know *all* the rules of the game. Trust me, this counts, or the lady wouldn't have given it to me."

"Who's the lady?"

"I'm not at liberty to say." I shoved the book under my arm, to prevent it from opening to the title page and the incriminating autograph. A homeless person stood a better chance of being admitted to Charleston society than a hack writer from Hackensack, New Jersey.

"You never did explain," Bob croaked, "how you choose the houses. Do these people know you're coming?"

"Oh, yes. It's all prearranged."

"But except for the pedigree, you haven't exactly hit pay dirt."

I sighed with mock impatience. "Yes, I have. These folks know to expect me, but they don't know what item it is I'll be requesting. That's the fun of it for them. I get points for creativity, you see."

"If you get points for that, you're a shoo-in," Rob said. He sounded only a mite sarcastic.

It was a good time to change the subject. "Lunch," I said. "Bob, didn't you say you were making something delicious for lunch?"

The way to a man's heart may or may not be through his stomach. It is definitely the way out of his head. The Rob-Bobs immediately quit obsessing about my bogus scavenger hunt, and began thinking about food.

Rob gave me a sly wink. "Actually, Abby, I was

able to talk Bob into saving our three-headed lunch for later. How does Magnolias sound?"

"Great," I replied, with a combination of relief at avoiding the planned menu and guilt at the memory of having stood Buford up two days earlier.

I smiled at the waiter, who looked uncannily like my son, Charlie. This fellow's name was Fritz. He had a Southern accent—Bavarian, I think.

"I'll start off with the Warm Oysters on the Half Shell with Andouille Sausage and Cheese Grits, Country Greens, Yellow Corn Salsa, and a Tomato Butter."

Fritz blinked.

"That's the second appetizer on the menu," I said helpfully.

"Abby," Rob groaned, "you're not going to do your shtick again where you read the entire description of each and every dish you order?"

"If Magnolias didn't want their menus read aloud, they shouldn't have made them sound so yummy. Fritz, dear, you ready?"

Fritz nodded.

"Good, because for the salad course I'll have the Grilled Portobello Mushroom Cap Layered with Fresh Tomato, Shaved Red Onion, Mashed Avocado, and Carolina Goat Cheese, Served with a Spicy Tomato Chutney."

Fritz scribbled.

"For my main course I'll have the six ounce Filet of Beef and Crabcake with Sautéed Spinach, Herb Fingerling Potatoes, Madeira Sauce, and Chive Mousseline."

"What the hell is a fingerling potato?" Rob demanded. For all his class, he's a French fry and hamburger sort of guy.

Bob blushed at his partner's question. "A fingerling—"

"Oh, my God! Look who just walked in!" I snatched up my heavily starched napkin and held it in front of my face like an Arabian veil.

Three heads swiveled. Rob turned back first.

"You can't hide, Abby. Even if you slid all the way under the table, he's bound to come over and say hello to Bob and me at some point."

There are two types of people in this world: those who know no fear (and they are not long for this world), and the rest of us. Of the rest of us, some of us like to confront our bogeymen head on, while others of us prefer to shiver under the covers (or behind napkins) until we have no choice. As a little girl, if I thought I heard something under the bed, I'd whip back the covers and jab at the space with a broom handle. Get it before it gets me, has always been my motto.

I seemed to have regressed a bit, but there was no

time like the present to regain my feistiness. I threw
down my napkin, shoved back my chair, and marched
across the room.

My friends moaned in tandem. I think Fritz
moaned as well. At any rate, I ignored them and
marched right up to my biggest source of fear.

"Buford!"

He appeared to be genuinely startled. Then again,
how does one read the expression on a snake?

"Abby!" He had just sat, but was on his feet in a
nanosecond. In his chest beat the cold-blooded heart
of a reptile, but he was, nonetheless, a Southern
gentleman.

"I'm sorry I stood you up," I blurted. "There were
extenuating circumstances."

"That's all right, Abby, I understand."

"You *do*?"

"Things come up, right?"

"Is that supposed to be a sexual reference?"

"What?"

"Never mind." I shifted from one size four to the
other. "Buford, what is it you wanted to talk to me
about?"

He gestured at the opposite chair. "Abby, won't
you join me? We can talk about it over lunch."

I pointed over my shoulder to the Rob-Bobs. "I've
already ordered. Thanks."

"We'll get the waiter to bring it over here."

"But—"

"Please, Abby, this is important."

I climbed on to the proffered seat. "Only until your drinks waiter gets back."

"Thanks, Abby."

"Spill," I said, giving the demon under my bed a good poke with the broom handle.

14

Buford folded his hands and looked at me under lids that had grown puffy over the years. What had once been a hunk of burning flesh was now a fluffy mound shaped only by an expensive summer suit.

"I have a daughter, Abby."

"Tell me about it. I was there, remember? Eight hours of labor—no drugs—because I didn't want Mama to say I'd wimped out. Thank God I wised up when Charlie was born."

"I'm not talking about Susan. I have another daughter. Heather."

I stared at my ex. Buford does not, never has had, a sense of humor. Still, we were living in an age of medical wonders, what with Rogaine, Viagra, and that new bra I read about that actually increases breast size.

"Was it surgically implanted?" I asked in all earnestness. "Or does it come in pill form?"

"What?"

"Your sense of humor."

"I'm not joking, Abby. While I was married—and don't get me wrong, I'm not proud of it—I had an affair."

The short hairs on the back of my neck stood up. I wanted to stand as well, but I wasn't sure my legs would hold me.

"During which marriage did you have this affair? I mean this *other* affair?"

"My marriage to Tweetie. Heather is two."

My sigh of relief caused a candle across the room to flicker. Buford had cheated on a dead woman. Well, perhaps she hadn't been dead then, but at least she wasn't still around to mind. You might wonder what difference it made to me whom Buford cheated on, given that we have been long divorced. All I can say is that it did make a difference. Perhaps it boils down to this; to be cheated on once makes me a victim of Buford's slimy nature, while being cheated on twice makes me a victim of my own stupidity. I would much rather be Buford's victim.

"Details," I said.

"She was an office manager in the law firm next to mine. You remember, White, Hammerhead & Lamprey. Anyway, she just told me last week that I was the father. Wait—" he took out a very flat and very expensive wallet—"here's a picture if you want to see."

"I don't."

He put the wallet away. "Somehow I didn't think

you would. But, Abby, just so you know, I plan to do right by this woman. I plan to marry her—give the kid a father."

"Uh-huh."

"No, I mean it. I'm a changed man."

I saw the drinks waiter coming and waited to speak until he was through serving Buford's martini. Having already ordered at my own table, I declined to place an order myself.

"And O.J. Simpson is looking hard for Nicole's killer," I said when the coast was clear. "Well, I've got news for you, Buford. He isn't going to find the killer unless he takes a mirror with him to the putting green."

"Are you trying to say you think I'm not capable of changing?"

"Bingo."

"Well, I am, and I'll prove it."

"Okay, okay, I believe you. Just tell me what this has to do with me."

"I need your advice, Abby."

"I think you should go ahead and have that vasectomy—the one you already claim to have had."

"I deserve that, Abby. I really was going to get one, but Tweetie changed her mind and said she might want children someday after all."

"Oh, you must be talking about vasectomy number two. Vasectomy number one supposedly happened while we were married."

He didn't even have the grace to blush. "Abby, enough about us. I want to talk about Susan and Charlie."

"What about them?"

"How do I go about telling them? Should I start with telling them about Loretta, and that I plan to marry her, or do I jump right in and tell them they have a sister?"

It wasn't until he said the S word that it really hit me. The tears poured out. Had I been sitting at my own table where I could see, although barely, that my appetizer was being served, I would have oversalted the food to compensate for my sudden loss of sodium. A sister! My children had a sister that was no part of me. For some strange reason that stung like a ton of salt on a skinned knee.

But that was all neither here nor there. I had my children to consider. Who was I to deny them a sister, or for that matter, her them? Besides, it would be only a matter of time before they found out anyway—unlike most lawyers, Buford's lips could sink a flotilla of ships. Where would I be then?

"Start with Loretta, Buford. Then work your way up to their baby sister. But it's going to come as a shock, no matter how you tell them."

"I know. I really just wanted to—uh, let you be the first to know."

In a weird way I understood that. Buford's parents are dead, and he has no siblings. If sharks have friends, then he has a few, but I doubt if he ever shares personal news with them. I was still family to Buford; someone he felt a need to connect with at one of life's pivotal moments.

I found myself smiling. "Thanks—I guess. But don't be surprised, Buford, if they take this hard."

He looked me straight in the eyes, and for a second I could see the Buford I fell in love with almost a quarter century ago. "Abby, I don't know where things went wrong—with us, I mean. I wish—uh— well, I wish we could get it back somehow. You don't suppose there is a chance? If this thing with Loretta doesn't work out?"

I slid to my feet. "Calista Flockhart will join Weight Watchers before that happens. Buford, because you're my children's father, and will someday be the grandfather of my grandchildren, I intend to be civil whenever we're together in public. But I would sooner crawl in bed with Saddam Hussein and an open bag full of snakes than get back together with you."

He nodded, apparently not in the least bit surprised. "Anyway, thanks for the advice, Abby. It was good seeing you again."

I scooted back to my own table before the Warm Oysters on the Half Shell turned cold.

The Rob-Bobs graciously allowed me to eat before grilling me. When they were quite through, and we'd

all had dessert—Mocha Crème Brulee with Fresh
Strawberries and an Orange Cinnamon Syrup—Rob
turned to me.

"You know, Abby, Bob and I aren't quite as stupid
as we look."

"Neither of you looks particularly stupid."

"Thanks. We're at least not so stupid that we think
you're on a legitimate scavenger hunt."

The lunch, which had tasted so good going down,
wasn't going to taste very good on its way back up.
"Whatever do you mean?" I said and batted my eye-
lashes.

Alas, my feminine wiles were wasted on the guys.
"Don't play games with us, Abby."

"You're not going to turn me in, are you?"

"We ought to," Bob boomed. Half the remaining
lunch crowd looked our way.

"But we won't," Rob said, "as long as you follow
our rules."

"Anything." Perhaps I'd spoken too soon. "What
are your rules?"

"Rule one. If you're caught, you have to deny this
conversation, or one like it, ever happened."

"Done."

"Rule two. As far as Rob and I are concerned, this
conversation never happened."

"That means no details," Bob bellowed. "We don't
want to know a thing. Because if anyone asks, we
know nothing."

Rob patted his partner's arm. "Finally, rule number three. If you get in over your head—that is to say, if it starts to feel at all uncomfortable—you bail out. Is that clear?"

"Yah vo, mein kommodant."

"Abby, we're not kidding around here. If you break these rules, we're driving you straight back to head-quarters. And Colonel Hogan won't be there to bail you out."

I should have been grateful that they were indulging me. In fact, I should have been flattered, because clearly it was a testament to their faith in my ability to ferret out the facts. However, what I should have felt, and what I felt, were quite different things. To put it frankly, I was pissed. I felt patronized.

"So Abby, do you swear?" Bob's voice is so loud that I had no doubt the entire restaurant, including the kitchen staff, could hear. While some may have thought I was being asked to give my word of honor, others might well have thought I was being asked if I cussed. It was most embarrassing.

"I swear," I said through gritted teeth. "And I swear if you don't lower your voice, I'm going to make a scene, the likes of which, you will never forget."

"Ooh, feisty," Rob said. "Abby, if I were straight—"

Bob's glare cut him short. Lunch was over.

Because I no longer needed to play games with the guys, I was free to rearrange the order of my visitations. Now, isn't that a much nicer word than interrogations? At any rate, I decided to get the longest drive out of the way by visiting Thelma Maypole down on Kiawah Island. However, in order to do that, I needed her to call the gate and leave my name. Twice. Thelma Maypole must have heeded her own investment counseling, because she lived in the heart of this posh resort community about forty minutes south of Charleston.

I needn't have worried. Anyone who comes all the way into town for social contact such as the Heavenly Hustlers has got to be more lonely than a petunia in an onion patch. Thelma Maypole not only agreed to let me visit, but invited me to spend the night.

"I have a spacious guest room," she said. "Actually, I have three. Although one is primarily a sewing room. Did you know that Elias Howe of Spencer, Massachusetts, got a patent on a sewing machine in 1846? Of course, Isaac Merritt Singer improved on the design, and by 1860 there were over a hundred thousand sewing machines produced in the United States alone."

"How fascinating. But I'll only be needing about a half hour of your time."

"Ah, the clock. The Egyptians, of course, made their famous water clocks, but the first mechanical clock, one that could strike on the hour, was made in Milan, Italy, in 1335."

"You don't say. Speaking of clocks, like I said, I can't stay very long."

Thelma sighed. She seemed genuinely disappointed. I allowed her to get over her disappointment by giving me directions and a not-so-very-brief history of Kiawah Island.

I will spare you the history of the island, but feel compelled to deliver a short geography lesson. South Carolina coastal islands are not what typically springs to mind when one hears the word island. Forget Tahiti and Bora Bora. Forget even the Bahamas. Yes, our islands have plenty of palm trees, but they are as flat as a putting green and are not set apart from the mainland by large expanses of water. Tidal creeks and salt marshes help define many of our islands, so that it is possible to drive from one island to another and not be aware that one is actually island-hopping.

We took River Road to Bohicket, passing under spreading oaks festooned with Spanish moss. The entrances to old plantations whizzed by, giving me just a tantalizing peek down allees of olive oaks and camellias as big as single-story houses. Beautiful as the scenery was, it seemed to take forever and a day to get to the bottom of Johns Island. Then we passed a small shopping center with a Piggly Wiggly and suddenly we were on Kiawah Island.

I have to hand it to the developers of this island paradise. Apart from the golf courses, the parts of the island I saw were still lush and heavily wooded. The large, expensive homes were tucked between ancient trees, seeming almost to be part of the landscape.

Thelma Maypole lived on Glen Abbey Drive, in a two-story cedar home that was all but lost among the trees. Like its neighbors, Thelma's house was set a full story above the ground to protect it from tidal surges. The wooden steps that led up to the teak-and-leaded-glass door were lined with terra-cotta pots of impatiens in red, white, and mauve. I could hear, but not see, water splashing in a fountain nearby, somewhere under the trees.

The Rob-Bobs had elected to walk to the beach, a short block away. Thelma, I'm sure, would have been delighted to meet them, but my friends were adamant about not learning anything more than they had to about my "case." They agreed to meet me in Thelma's driveway in thirty minutes. If I needed more time, I was to appear at the door and wave.

If Thelma saw the Rob-Bobs get out of the car and stroll away, she made no mention of it.

"I was afraid you might have gotten lost," she said, as she opened the door. "The roads tend to wind a bit. But then you should see the road from the Granada to Almunecar. That's in Spain, you know. It crosses the Sierra Nevada mountains, which reach a height of eleven thousand four—"

"Sorry if it took me longer than you thought it would. It was such a beautiful drive. And speaking of beautiful, your home is exquisite."

I meant it. Thelma Maypole had good-quality furniture, but most of the pieces were not antique. It was the abundance of artifacts, some ingeniously displayed, that showed this was the home of a woman who had been somewhere, and learned something unusual in her spare time.

On the expanse of wall opposite the fireplace hung a seven-foot silk *uchikake*, a Japanese wedding kimono. Since few Japanese women are that tall, the garment was obviously meant to be dragged, rather like a bridal train. This particular piece was red-orange silk, with black and white embroidered cranes, and a good deal of gold thread for accent. It was breathtaking.

The contemporary Italian marble and carved mahogany coffee table, probably from Haverty's, served as a display surface for a variety of objets d'art. The most interesting of these pieces was an unusually large tile set on an inexpensive easel, the sort you might pick up at Pottery Barn. The tile depicted a crude rendition of a monkey munching on a pomegranate.

"I see you've been to Portugal," I said.

Thelma Maypole nodded. Her hexagonal glasses reflected the many colors and shapes around her, turning the lenses into kaleidoscopes.

"I've been to twenty-three countries. I could show you my passport if you like—all those visa stamps. Did you know that to get into Albania—"

"But you've been to Portugal?" I know it's rude to

interrupt. But isn't it equally as rude to allow a long-winded person to wear herself out?

"Ah, yes, Portugal. The last good bargain in Europe. A lot of tourists head straight to the Algarve, and the beaches in the south. But the Lisbon area has so many museums, so many treasures. We could have stayed there longer—skipped the trip south, if only Francis hadn't been so stubborn."

"Francis?"

"Dr. Francis Lloyd Whipperspoonbill." She clapped chubby unadorned hands to bare, chubby cheeks. "Gracious me! I seem to have forgotten my manners. Would you care for something to drink?"

"Tempt me," I said. I was still satiated from my scrumptious lunch at Magnolias, and more in need of a restroom than anything else. Experience has taught me never to pass up a clean toilet, or a free beverage.

"Well, let's see. I have sweet tea, diet cola, orange juice, some claret—"

"Claret," I declared.

While she fetched the wine, I checked out the powder room. It was unremarkable, except for the Luba carvings from Africa displayed casually on a wicker shelf. They were of the finest quality, and deserved a better venue. On the other hand, what better place to sit and contemplate a work of art?

When I returned to the great room, Thelma handed me a glass. "As I'm sure you know, claret is just another term for any of the numerous wines from the

Bordeaux region of France. Although originally claret meant a pale wine that was a mixture of red and white. That dates back to the twelfth century—"

I should have my mouth taped shut, but I interrupted her again. "Cheers," I said, waving my glass aloft. "Now, tell me about your trip to Portugal with Dr. Whipperspoonbill."

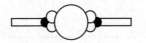

15

She must have blinked behind the bizarre lenses, because the twin kaleidoscopes exhibited a flurry of activity. "Well, I wasn't there with just him. The entire group went along."

"What group would that be?"

"Why, the Heavenly Hustlers, of course."

"When was this?"

"Two years ago in May."

"That would be before Mama joined."

She nodded. "Mozella would have been a wonderful addition to the trip. Francis—well, all he cared about was the beaches. Wanted to see if the ladies went topless, I suppose, like they do on the Riviera. Can you blame me for breaking off our engagement?"

I swallowed more claret than I'd intended. "You were engaged to each other?"

Thelma Maypole patted the gray wedge of hair on the left side of her head. "We were engaged for three years," she said, then lapsed into uncharacteristic silence.

I waited for her to continue. I couldn't imagine a union between her and Dr. Francis Lloyd Whipperspoonbill. On the other hand, I couldn't imagine either of them married to anyone else.

"The institution of marriage," she finally said, "has been found to exist in all societies, past and present. The ancient Romans recognized three types of marriage: one for the patrician class, one for the plebeians, and one for slaves. In patrician families the event was called *confarreatio* and marked by—"

I raised my glass of claret. "To marriage!"

She raised her glass as well, and took a sip. "Francis was fine with our engagement, but backed out of getting married." She chugged the rest of our wine. "At the last *minute*. He literally left me standing at the altar."

"Oh, my."

She nodded, making me dizzy with the resultant light show. "At St. Michaels, no less," she said, referring to one of the nation's most historical churches, which happens to be in Charleston. The building was constructed in 1752, and George Washington, the Marquis de Lafayette, and Robert E. Lee all attended services there.

"That must have been embarrassing."

"It was beyond embarrassing. We had eight hundred guests, including the governor of South Carolina. Francis is well-connected, you see. At any rate, there I was, having just been walked down the aisle by my daddy, who was ninety-two at the time, when Francis backed out. And like I said, I meant that literally. He walked backward to a side door. That's the last anyone saw of him that day." She laughed briefly. "Well, Mama and Daddy were raised during the Depression, and since Daddy was paying for the wedding—Mama's been dead since 'eighty-three—we went right on with the reception, which was held in the Exchange Building. And then, because our tickets to Aruba were nonrefundable, I went on my honeymoon. With Daddy—well, not *with* Daddy, but you know what I mean. We had the best time, probably even better than I would have had if Francis had been along instead."

"You go, girl!"

She sighed heavily. "That is, until Daddy died."

"I'm so sorry!"

"Don't be. He died on the way home. Fell asleep in first class and never woke up."

"We should all be that lucky."

"Exactly. Still, I can't help but think that Daddy might be alive today if Francis hadn't stood me up. That unexpected vacation was a little hard on Daddy, especially all those late nights in the casinos."

"I can't believe you still belong to the same club as Dr. Whipperspoonbill." I suppose I could have called the man Francis—he couldn't hear me, after all—but

I loved the workout his name gave my lips. Heck, saying it three times in a row was practically as good as a collagen injection.

Thelma looked down at her empty glass. "It's like following through with the reception and the trip to Aruba. Living well is the best revenge. Isn't that what they say? I figure the best way to come out ahead is to act as if Francis never hurt me."

Now this was a wise woman. I wish I'd done that when Buford dumped me—although my circumstances were quite a bit different. For all intents and purposes he'd had our son taken away from me, not to mention my home.

"How does Francis act, if you don't mind my asking?"

"That's the maddening part. He doesn't act any differently. It's like nothing ever happened."

"And you're all right with that?"

"Of course not. But if I let on that I'm hurt or angry, then he wins, doesn't he?"

I nodded. We all do what works for us, and because I understand that, I try to make allowances for people whenever I can. But palling around with someone who had embarrassed me in front of family and friends, not to mention Charleston society, was beyond my ken. Passing judgment on Thelma Maypole, however, was not why I'd gotten the Rob-Bobs to drive me all the way down to Kiawah Island.

"The night of the séance—did you see anyone go into the dining room alone?"

She stared at me. I couldn't see her eyes, but I could tell she wasn't even blinking. No aurora borealis.

"Well?" I asked patiently. Time was getting away from me, and the Rob-Bobs were due back any minute.

"Abby—may I call you that?"

"By all means."

"Abby—you know it's funny, come to think of it, but I live on Glen Abbey Drive. Although why it is named that is beyond me. Strictly speaking a glen is a narrow, secluded valley, while an abbey is a monastery governed by an abbot. And since there are no proper valleys here on Kiawah—"

"The séance," I said, perhaps a bit too sharply. "Who was alone in the dining room that night?"

"Francis," she said softly.

"You sure?"

"Quite. I was on my way back to the kitchen to get another of those delicious ham and biscuit sandwiches when I noticed him standing hunched over the table, his buttocks toward the door."

"What was he doing?"

"I couldn't see. But I spoke his name and he straightened and turned—whirled actually. It was like I caught him at something."

"Did you mention this to anyone?"

"As a matter of fact, yes. I mentioned it—casually, mind you—to your mother."

"Mama? Why her?"

"Well, I thought someone should know. But Abby, please don't think I'm telling you this to get back at Francis in any way. That sort of getting even is not my style."

"I understand totally," I said. There were, indeed, many things I understood totally. But Thelma Maypole and her continued association with Dr. Francis Lloyd Whipperspoonbill was not among them.

We chatted for a few more minutes. That is say, she began a lengthy geological description of the Carpathian Mountains. The only reason I didn't cut her off at the pass was that I was trying to figure out how she'd made the switch to such an esoteric subject. I never did make the connection, but I came to my senses and beat a hasty retreat. When I got to the car the Rob-Bobs were already in it, looking as glum as if they'd both been stood up at the altar.

"Let me get this straight," I said. "Y'all are pissed at each other because you both made goo-goo eyes at a cute guy on the beach."

"I wasn't looking at him," Rob said. "I was admiring his swim trunks. They were Calvin Klein."

"It wasn't his trunks you were admiring," Bob boomed.

Rob slapped the steering wheel with an open palm.

"You're the one who pointed him out. Said he looked like Tom Cruise."

I tried in vain to whistle with two fingers in my mouth. "Guys!" I finally shouted. "Give it a rest. What if I carried on like that about some stranger I'd seen?"

Rob glanced at me. "Abby, I hate to remind you, but before you married Greg, you walked around with your tongue hanging out half the time."

"I did not!"

Bob's basso profundo made me jump. "You did so."

"At least I gave it up when I got married. You two have each other, it's the same thing."

They were silent for a few miles. "Where to next?" Rob asked when we were well off the island, and headed back up Bohicket Road.

"I don't know the address for this one, so we need to stop at a gas station so I can look it up. All I know is his name, Whipperspoonbill." I bit my lip. "Oops, I just broke Rule Number Three, didn't I? No details."

Bob cleared his throat. "Uh—there can't be that many Whipperspoonbills, can there?"

I didn't know to whom he was addressing the question, but I took the liberty of answering. The cat was already out of the bag, wasn't it?

"This is Dr. Francis Lloyd Whipperspoonbill. He's a veterinarian, not a people doctor."

Rob slowed the car. "Abby, we know this guy."

"You do?"

"We were at a party at his house just last week."

"Bald head on top? Speaks like he has lockjaw?"

"That's him all right."

"Get out of town!"

"It was a coming-out party," Bob said.

"He has a daughter in cotillion? I knew he was a widower, but I'd pegged him for older than that."

"Not that kind of coming-out party," Rob said. "Francis is gay."

"Oh. Well, that certainly explains some things."

"Like what?" Someone was owed yet another Coke.

"I'm not allowed to tell you, remember? No details."

"Abby," Rob said sternly, "this is different."

"No, it isn't. You just want to hear gossip."

"Please," Bob begged.

I threw up my hands in mock resignation. "Okay, but if I break this rule, then the whole deal is off. Rules One and Two go out the window as well."

We drove about another mile in silence. A pregnant sea turtle could have made better time up that highway. Rob finally pulled over to the shoulder to let an SUV pass.

"Okay," he said. "But there has to be a new rule— one where we all keep mum."

"Deal." I signed locking my lips and throwing away the key. It was such a juvenile gesture that had a mime done it, within my reach, I would have slapped him. It has always been my fantasy to slap a mime— but I digress.

"So spill, Abby."

I dutifully filled the guys in on my conversation with Thelma Maypole.

The Rob-Bobs wanted to come in with me when I called on Dr. Whipperspoonbill, but I refused to let them. Their presence would change the dynamics of the situation, possibly even removing certain elements of surprise. Since the veterinarian lived within a stone's throw of their own house, they parked in their driveway and I hoofed it over.

There was a genteel shabbiness about Francis Lloyd Whipperspoonbill's house. The eaves needed sanding and repainting, and several of the wooden hurricane shutters had slats missing. The minuscule lawn needed cutting, the shrubs needed pruning, and the wrought iron patio furniture was peeling and could, at the least, use a good hosing down. In another part of town—say, north of Broad—the word derelict might creep to, but not necessarily out of, one's lips. Three blocks back from South Battery, one could afford to be forgiving.

The doorbell also seemed to be out of commission, so I knocked with a ring suspended from the jaws of a bronze lion head. My timid taps went unanswered, so I gave the brass receiving plate a couple of hard raps before giving up. I was halfway down the steps when I heard the door open.

"Mrs. Washburn, is that you?"

I turned. Thelma Maypole's former fiancé was standing in the doorway, wearing his striped cotton seersucker suit and silk bow tie. I scrambled back up the steps, and as I got closer I could see that he was wearing his white bucks as well. Dr. Francis Lloyd Whipperspoonbill was a true Charleston gentleman at home, as well as out. The only thing missing was the white straw hat, which, of course, would have been bad manners to wear indoors.

"Sir, I was wondering if I might have a few minutes of your time."

"By all means," he said, without moving his lips. "Please, come inside."

I did as bade and stepped into the previous century. No—make that even earlier. Everything was Victorian, from the dark heavy drapes to the carved and curved furniture with lace doilies pinned to strategic places. Even the dust was Victorian. I didn't know how the late Mrs. Whipperspoonbill died, but suffocation would have been my guess. It occurred to me that the reason the doctor spoke through clenched teeth was to avoid ingesting a mouthful of dust mites.

"Would you care for a drink?" my impromptu host asked, after I'd chosen what looked to be the cleanest chair.

"No thank you, I'm fine." The truth is I would have leaped at the offer under more hygienic circumstances.

"Well then, what can I do for you?"

"I'll come straight to the point, doctor. The night of the séance—did you see anyone alone in the dining room before it began?"

He stiffened. "No. I don't recall seeing anyone in there. Why do you ask?"

I stiffened as well. I hadn't intended to be so direct, and I certainly didn't expect him to give tit for tat.

"Well—uh—okay, doctor, I won't play games. My friend Jane Cox can't sleep because the police haven't figured out who Madame Woo-Woo's killer is. Since I'm married to a former detective, and have had a little experience in these matters, I thought I'd give them a helping hand. Unofficially, by the way." That last was meant for my protection, as well as his comfort level.

"Like I said, I didn't see anyone in the dining room. Not until Mozella—your mother—called us in with her interpretation of a town crier."

"That was amusing, wasn't it? However, Dr. Whipperspoonbill—and I don't mean to put you on the spot here—somebody did say that they saw you in there."

"Who?" His lips actually opened.

"Thelma Maypole."

"Oh, her." He was back to playing ventriloquist. "She would say that."

"Why? Does she have a bone to pick with you?"

"Don't play games with me, Mrs. Washburn. I'm

sure she told you about the wedding fiasco. And no doubt she embellished the story."

"She did indeed tell me, but I have no idea whether she embellished it or not."

"Would you care to hear the truth?"

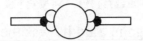

16

"I'd love to hear your version."

He frowned. "You're a clever woman, Mrs. Washburn."

"Thanks. Too bad my ninth grade algebra scores didn't reflect that."

The frown softened. "May I begin my account?"

"Yes, please."

He'd been standing, and before continuing he selected a chair. When he sat the air was filled with motes.

"Thelma and I were engaged for three years, although it seemed like ten. She's the one who kept postponing the wedding, not me. Then when she finally committed to the ceremony and we started making plans—well, can you believe she wanted her daddy along on our honeymoon to Aruba?"

"Hmm."

"Then the night of the rehearsal dinner she got dead drunk, and guess who she toasted?"

"A former boyfriend?"

"Her daddy again. Said he was the only man she'd ever truly loved, and would probably ever love."

"Ouch."

"Of course she said a lot of other crazy things too—because like I said, she was really drunk. So anyway, I thought I'd chalk it all up to the alcohol, but then when she was two hours late for the actual ceremony—well, can you blame me for having second thoughts?"

"You mean *she* stood *you* up?"

"I waited at the empty church—everyone else had long since gone home—because I felt that if I was patient long enough, she would somehow show up. In the meantime tourists came in and out. They probably thought I was nuts standing there in my tuxedo. Finally Thelma did show up—with her daddy, of course. She was wearing her wedding gown, but she looked—well, disgusting. Like she'd been sleeping in it or something. You can bet she was still hung over."

"Wow. I'll say this, y'all's stories don't jibe at all."

"Well, I have witnesses—a whole church full of them. At least for the first hour."

I nodded. "In that case, let me ask you this—and it's the same question I asked her. Why did you stay a member of the Heavenly Hooters—I mean, Hustlers—after that? Didn't you hate her guts?"

"Not really. To tell you the truth, I felt sorry for her. Besides, it was her daddy's money that was wasted, not mine. I hear that the reception food was donated to a homeless shelter, so I guess somebody actually benefited."

"Still, you Hustlers must be a tight little bunch."

He cocked his head to consider the validity of my statement. The light from a dusty rose Victorian lampshade cast a strangely appealing glow on his bald pate.

"We are. Except for your mother, we've known each other for years. Palled around. It's hard to make friends these days—you don't want to dump the ones you have."

"But you grew up here. In Charleston."

"Yes, but you lose friends—to death—or they move away. And I guess some folks just find it easier to make friends than others."

That's when I did something terribly inappropriate. Just for having brought up the subject, I should be slapped by a hundred mimes, none of them wearing gloves.

"From what I hear," I said, "you've been making new friends lately."

The color of his pate deepened to a brick red. "What do you mean?"

"Uh—nothing."

"Wait just one minute. You're friends with Rob Goldburg and Bob Steuben, aren't you? I should have known."

"Busted," I said.

"Well, for your information, Mrs. Washburn, I am not a—well, I am not gay, as they say these days."

"Your sexual orientation is none of my business, doctor. And I apologize for having even gone there. I must say your reaction surprises me, however. From what I hear, Charleston is a fairly tolerant city, as long as one doesn't confront anyone directly with one's lifestyle. You know, get in their face."

His pate was still an unnatural red. "The party was for a young friend of mine, not me. I can see now that it was a huge mistake." He stood. "Mrs. Washburn, I will not allow my reputation to be tarnished."

I stood as well. "It's unfortunate, doctor, that you think one's sexual orientation—one way or the way—can somehow be tarnishing. It's not like committing a crime. It's not murder."

He didn't appear to be listening. "That Madame Woo-Woo was a fraud. Everyone knew it. If someone hadn't murdered her, I would have sued."

It was time to abandon my wagon, and jump into his. It promised to be a more interesting ride.

"Sued her for what?"

"We had this group reading—that's what led to the séance, you know. Everyone was impressed with her. Why shouldn't they be? The Riffles were told they were going to make a million-dollar profit on some ridiculous car. Ella was going to hit the *New York Times* best-seller list. Thelma was going to meet a tall, dark, handsome stranger and—"

"And Mama?" I asked anxiously.

"She was finally going to get the great-grandchild she's been wanting."

"Not on your life! Not anytime soon. Neither Susan nor Charlie are married."

"Like I said, she was a fraud."

I remembered whose wagon I was riding in. "What about you? What did she predict for you?"

The pate faded to an ashy pink and he studied a doily on the arm of a chair. "The same thing she told Thelma."

"That you would meet a tall, dark, handsome stranger?"

He cringed. "Ella Nolte is a writer. They repeat everything—put it in their books. What you said before—about not advertising your personal business. My friends, I can trust. Ella Nolte is another matter."

"I thought she was your friend. Isn't that what the Heavenly Hustlers is all about?"

"Yes, but you know what I mean."

I said good-bye. I did indeed know what he meant. Dr. Francis Lloyd Whipperspoonbill, not unlike the rest of us, had more than one circle of friends. The various circles were not intended to intertwine. Madame Woo-Woo's prediction had sounded an embarrassing note in the wrong circle.

"Do you think the doc is capable of murder?" I asked. It was a silly question. I believe anyone to be capable of the act, given the right circumstances. And even though we were no longer playing by the rules, I knew the Rob-Bobs were not about to incriminate a friend.

"Abby," Rob said, "you know we're not going to answer that. But I will tell you this. It was that Maypole woman who stood Francis up on the wedding day, not the other way around."

"How do you know for sure? You weren't even living in Charleston then. Or did you already know Dr. Whipper-what's-his name somehow?"

Bob felt the need to exercise his bass. "Abby, we don't know every gay man in America. It's not like there's a national roster. But we share mutual friends with Francis. Some of them were there—discreetly, of course. They told us what happened."

"So, that means Thelma Maypole out-and-out lied. She's trying to frame him."

"That would seem to be the case," Rob said. He turned the corner. We were somewhere up in North Charleston, in one of the less-desirable parts of that fair city. All I knew was that the Northwoods Mall was somewhere to my left, and that if my next two interviews went quickly, there might still be time to hit the handbag sale at Dillard's and get home before Greg. I know, most women prefer a shoe sale, but when one wears a size four, like I do, the selection is limited. Purses, on the other hand, seldom have to fit body parts.

"Good God," Bob boomed suddenly, "the woman lives in a double-wide."

"*Lived*," I said. "Madame Woo-Woo is dead. It's her boyfriend who lives here. But you're right, it is a mobile home."

We pulled into a sandy driveway. A strip of weeds ran down the middle, making it look like a safari track. Overgrown photinias and a plethora of pittosporums added to the jungle affect. It was not the kind of place one would picture a successful psychic living.

"Maybe you've got the wrong address, Abby."

I consulted what I'd scribbled down from the Yellow Pages. "No, this is it. Perhaps this is just her office."

The men declined to walk with me to the door, but they also refused to drop me off and head out to the mall on their own. Rob parked in the shade of a live oak and turned off the engine. They would wait, they said. If I was admitted into the trailer—which they claimed was no bigger than the *Hunley*, despite it being a double-wide—Rob would activate his gold stopwatch. Ten minutes was all I had. If I wasn't back outside in ten minutes, they were calling the cops.

They meant ten minutes from the time I disappeared inside the metal home, not from the moment I got out of the car. Just to get their goats, I did the Charleston walk up the sandy lane. That is to say, I ambled—the way one is supposed to walk on a hot sultry day. Can I help it if my legs are a bit on the short side, and at full speed, can barely outrun a glacier? (I haven't done a whole lot of that, mind you, so this is mostly conjecture.)

At last I reached a set of rickety wooden steps, and taking my life into my hands climbed them. Risking tetanus, I pressed the rusty doorbell. The flimsy aluminum door was flung open at once.

"Get the hell out of here, or I'm calling the police."

"Call away," I said, calling his bluff. Somehow I got the idea that the shirtless young man in baggy shorts with more tattoos than a bar full of bikers, was not about to get the police involved for no good reason.

"What is it you want?"

I wanted to ask him why the waistband of his shorts was halfway down his buttocks, and if he minded looking as if his diaper needed changing. I wanted to inform him that this bizarre fashion statement, once so popular, was now on the wane—even here in the hinterlands of South Carolina. Alas, good breeding, coupled with common sense, prevented me from being so rude. The half-dropped drawers could well be concealing a handgun. Maybe even a couple of sticks of dynamite.

"I'm a friend of Golda Feinstein," I said, lying through my teeth. Fortunately falsehoods do not contribute to caries.

I could tell by his reaction that he'd been blindsided. He stared hard at me, which gave me a perfectly good excuse to stare back. He was surprisingly

young—hardly more than a teenager. It seems that
Madame Woo-Woo had robbed the cradle.

"Name's Ben," he finally said, extending his hand.
Then he snatched it back. I think he did so out of
nerves, rather than nastiness.

"Abigail Washburn. I'd like to ask you a few questions, if it's all right."

He glanced around me. I knew he could see the car,
despite the jungle. But could he see the two men in it?

"You sure you're not the police?"

"Positive! Why, just look at me—the police have
minimum height requirements, you know."

"Are you a reporter?"

"What? And work for the enemy? Like I said,
Golda was my friend."

He studied me again. "My sister didn't have many
friends, and she never mentioned you. But what the
hell, come on in."

Sister? The two of them looked nothing alike, even
if you took into account Golda's gypsy wig. But then,
who was I to jump to such hasty conclusions? My
brother Toy is six feet tall and blond, just like our
daddy was.

I followed Ben into the dimly lit but surprisingly
well-appointed trailer. Who would have suspected
that a North Charleston doublewide would be furnished with nineteenth-century pieces, primarily in
the Empire style? Madame Waterloo would have
been a better name for the deceased seer.

"This is very nice," I said. I wasn't being conde-
scending.

"Thanks, it was our mother's."

"She has good taste." I remembered to look at my
watch.

"She was an antique dealer. So was our father. But
they're both dead now. They were killed in a car
wreck on I-95 just outside of Ridgeville, South Carolina. We were moving from New York to Florida,
and Sis got the moving van to drop everything off
here. Neither of us wanted to go to Florida in the first
place, and we'd already said our good-byes in New
York. Anyway, that was five years ago—no make that
six. Golda's been looking out for me ever since then.
Not that I need it any more. I'm twenty-two."

I couldn't continue lying to an orphan, even one
who was proud of his age. "I have a confession to
make, I'm really not—"

"A friend of Golda's?" He smiled, and a dragon
that started on his chest, head down, wiggled the tip
of its tail across Ben's right cheek.

"But I did meet her once," I wailed. "The night she
was murdered."

The M word seemed to hit him hard and he sat
heavily on a chair fit for Napoleon. A second later he
motioned me to sit as well.

"So, you're one of the Heavenly Hoofers," he said.

"That's Hustlers, and no, I'm not one of them. My

mama is. The séance was at my best friend's house—but you have to believe me when I say she didn't do it."

His eyes narrowed as the dragon tail twitched. "How can you be sure?"

"I know what you mean, and I'd normally say that I can't be sure. But Jane Cox has the heart of a puppy dog and absolutely no motive. I was hoping that you might have some ideas."

"Like who might have it in for my sister?"

"Exactly."

"Dissatisfied customers, that's who."

"How so?"

"Let's say you went to my sister to have your fortune told, and she predicted you were going to lose your job and go bankrupt. And then it happens. Well, you know what they say about killing the messenger."

"Just for the record, I'm self-employed and well in the black—but I see your point. Did that kind of thing happen a lot?"

He bit his lip, tugging at the tip of the dragon's tail. "More often than you'd think. That's why we took the sign down. We asked to be dropped from the Yellow Pages, but of course that takes a year."

"She planned to go out of business?"

"Golda had built up a base of reliable customers, you see—and then there was the ghost-busting. Almost no one complains about that."

I looked at my watch. I was running out of time.

"You knew about the Heavenly Hustlers. Did she have problems with any of them?"

"None that I know of. They came here once for a group reading. But whenever Sis had clients, I hid out in the back bedroom and watched TV. Unless, of course, I had plans, because hey, I'm not a couch potato."

The dragon and other mythical characters that covered his body did nothing to hide his splendid physique. I'd been trying not to look, but just to confirm what he said, I sneaked a peek.

"I believe you, Ben." I stood, and took one last look around. "Your parents knew a lot about antiques."

"Yeah. Golda, too. She really liked this shit—uh, I mean stuff. Me? I'd just as soon have a La-Z-Boy recliner and a six-pack—if you know what I mean."

"I think I do. I have a son in college. What do you do for a living, Ben? Or are you in school?"

"I work at a car wash. I'm fixing to make assistant manager in six months if I don't screw up." He paused and gazed down at bare feet. "Hey, you want me to let you know when the funeral is? The police—well, they have to keep her a while longer. But they said maybe by Friday."

"Sure, I'd like that."

"And the rest of them—the Hustlers—you'll tell them too, right?"

"Absolutely."

We shook hands, but just as I was turning to leave, a small gold-framed photo on an end table caught my eye. I walked over to examine it. At first I couldn't believe my eyes.

17

"Who is that?" I demanded.

"Chiz. Golda's boyfriend."

"Chisholm Banncock, the hoity-toity real estate agent?"

He shrugged. "Never asked what he did. I just know him as Chiz. He and Golda were pretty tight—always wanting their space. Like I said, I hung out a lot in the back bedroom."

"Wow! That's incredible—I mean, that really surprises me, what with Chiz coming from—uh, the old guard." Even a size four foot is more than a mouthful.

"The man's a bastard. What he did to Golda was unforgiveable."

"Hang on!" I cried. I dashed to the rickety front steps and flashed fingers. I couldn't allow the Rob-Bob SWAT team to storm the place just when I was getting somewhere. Back inside, I grabbed the framed photo. "Go on, Ben. Tell me what this skunk did."

"He strung Sis along, that's what. Got what he wanted—made her believe he was going to marry her, and then dumped her. And do you know why?"

Of course I did, but it was better to let him say it.
"Why?"

"Because we're Yankees. More than that, we're
poor Yankees."

"If it's any comfort, Ben, even a rich Southerner,
one from someplace else, would still have a hard time
marrying into that crowd. There are exceptions—perhaps more today than there used to be—but they're
still exceptions."

"Yeah, well, a poor Yankee is at the bottom of the
list, right?"

"I'm afraid so." It was almost true. Only a poor
black Yankee would be lower on that list.

He took the picture from me. "I'm throwing this
piece of shit away. Don't know why Sis hung on to it."

"A broken heart takes time to heal," I said ventur-
ing my woman's opinion. "Sometimes we think that
if we wait long enough, the guy will come to his
senses."

"Yeah? Well, he didn't have any sense if you ask
me. Sis was really cool. She would have made any
guy a good wife. Hell, she would have made a damn
good mom to some little kid. Maybe a bunch of
them."

Then it occurred to me. "Ben, was she—uh—was
there any chance she might have been expecting."

"Expecting what?"

"A baby. Could she have been pregnant?"

The dragon tattoo turned an ominous red, while the skin around it paled. "Never thought of that. I think they were using something—but it's not like we talked about it."

"Ben—"

"Hey, you don't think Chiz killed her, do you? I mean, he was there that night, right?"

"He was definitely there that night. And if she was pregnant—well, that looks like a motive to me."

"I'm calling the goddamn police," he said. "You can bet on that. I'm going to get me some answers."

"Ask for Sergeant Scrubb. But don't tell him I was here."

"Scrubb," he said, and wrote it down. "Hey thanks, Miss—uh—"

"Washburn. And remember, don't tell the police I was here. I'm in enough trouble as it is."

"No sweat." He didn't seem in the least bit curious about my trouble. Then again, he was only twenty-two.

"Well, good-bye."

"Yeah. And you're coming to the service, right?"

I said I would.

The Rob-Bobs ought never rib me again for changing my mind. They were dying to hear what had transpired in the trailer, and were both repulsed and fascinated by my description of Ben.

"I dated a man with a tattoo once," Rob said,

sounding almost wistful. "It was a lion with five—not four, but five—"

"Don't want to hear it!" Bob bellowed.

"Well, guys," I said, happy to referee, "either of you ever been to a car dealership called Cars of the Stars on Rivers Avenue?"

The men exchanged looks. Clearly, I'd caught them with their manicured fingers in the cookie jar.

"I was there only once," Rob said.

"Well, I'd like to go there next."

"And it was Bob's idea," Rob said, unable to leave well enough alone.

"*My* idea? You're the one who wanted to see the car where Paul Lynde lost his virginity."

"He lost it in a car?" I asked. "How do you know?"

"I don't," Rob said. "I just made it up. My point is, those cars are intriguing."

"I won't be looking at any cars," I snapped.

And I tried not to. There was a bright Porsche with a bullet hole in the windshield on the driver's side. I thought I remembered seeing that same car in *People* magazine.

While the Rob-Bobs satiated their ghoulish appetites, I found Hugh Riffle. It wasn't easy. Delbert, the salesman who pounced on me when I arrived like a chicken on a June bug, was bent on not letting me speak with his boss. In fact, he insisted his boss wasn't on the premises. But the fervor with which he said it convinced me otherwise, forcing me to employ the universal language: *money.* I slipped the dapper dandy enough dinero to keep him supplied with Minoxidil for a year. He led me straight to the holy of holies.

Actually, it looked more like somebody's garage. It was an enormous room containing six vintage automobiles. Five of the cars were, presumably, the real thing. The sixth was really a desk, in the shape of a car. It had no windshield, of course, so that the hood could be used to write on.

Hugh Riffle saw me approaching and grinned. That is to say, his jowls parted slightly and I could see teeth.

"Please tell me you decided to take me up on my offer."

"Offer?"

"You know, a little R and R in the sack."

He said that right in front of Delbert, if you can believe that. I hardly could. Delbert, however, acted as if Hugh Riffle was inquiring about the weather.

"I most certainly did not come here for that."

"Ah, a car. I've got just the thing for you. I just got in a replica of the car Jayne Mansfield died in. Just came in today. Of course it doesn't have the damage, and it's not the real thing—"

"I came to talk about Madame Woo-Woo."

"The dead psychic?"

"The murdered psychic," I said.

"Delbert," Hugh barked.

The salesman scampered from the room. If he'd been a dog, he would have had his tail between his legs.

Hugh motioned for me to sit in what I would swear was the bucket seat from a 1973 Camaro. I know, because Buford had one of those, and that's where I lost—uh, an earring.

"Now then," Hugh said, "what's this about Madame Woo-Woo? The police find out who killed her?"

"Not yet, but they're working on it."

"Then what's to talk about?"

"Look, I'll get straight to the point. Did you see anyone alone in the dining room the night of the séance—before my mama called everyone in with her embarrassing town-crier act?"

"No, and I didn't look. There wasn't any food in there, was there?"

I sighed. "It was all in the kitchen."

"Abby—mind if I call you that?"

"Well, frankly—"

"Abby, you shouldn't be bothering your pretty little head with stuff like this. Let the police handle it. In the meantime, you and I can handle each other—if you know what I mean."

"I have a fairly good idea, and I find it disgusting." I stood. "Good-bye, Mr. Riffle."

The jowls worked harder and I saw more teeth. "Touchy little thing, aren't you?"

Even a well-bred Southern gal has her breaking

point. "You're a sleazeball, Mr. Riffle. I wouldn't look twice at you if you were the last man on earth. No woman in her right mind would."

The teeth receded. "Not all women share your sentiments, little lady."

"Oh, yeah? Name one—besides your wife."

"Golda Feinstein. Now that was a hot piece of tail."

"*Excuse* me?"

"Madame Woo-Woo."

"I know who she *is*—uh, was. Are you saying you slept with her?"

"Does Marlon Brando like to eat?"

"I'll take that as a 'yes.' Well, Mr. Riffle, you just confirmed what I said. You're a sleazeball, all right."

"Hey, in this case it was her idea."

"I find that impossible to believe."

"Suit yourself. But she came to me—all red-eyed and crying, because her boyfriend broke up with her. I saw it as my duty to comfort the poor girl."

"Sheesh!" The man was full of himself. Whatever did Mama see in this band of misfits? Come to think of it, what did Hugh Riffle get out of belonging to this group? I decided to ask him.

My question seemed to be anticipated. "Oh, that's easy," he said, without missing a beat. "Companionship. We do things together. We have good times."

"It sounds like you have enough good times without the Heavenly Hustlers."

"Nah, it isn't the same. These people are my friends. We have stuff to talk about. You don't get that with a young piece of tail."

"You're disgusting, you know that?" I caught my breath as a frightening thought popped into mind. "You don't hit on my mother, do you?"

He had the temerity to laugh. "I don't bother with old gray mares—not when there's plenty of fillies around."

I turned heel and stamped out of the room. You can bet I slammed the door as hard as I could.

I found the Rob-Bobs examining a car in which a thousand pounds of heroin had been found by state troopers a year earlier. The vehicle had never been owned by a celebrity, at least not in the conventional sense, but it had made national news. The drugs, you see, had somehow been molded into the likenesses of people, and then dressed in clothes. A concerned citizen called the police when, at a roadside rest area, she noticed a car in which three of the passengers were staring straight ahead, as if in a trance.

"So how did it go?" my friends asked in unison.

"The man's a creep. Turns out he was sleeping with Golda Feinstein when she was on the rebound."

The Rob-Bobs shuddered. It was hard to say what they thought more repulsive, the thought of sleeping with Golda, or Hugh Riffle.

"Do you think she could have been blackmailing him?" Rob asked.

"I hadn't thought of that! But you know, you could be right. Or she could have been doing it to get back at Chiz—for dumping her. That's it. I've got to talk to Chiz Banncock next."

"But you already spoke with him, Abby. This morning."

"No, I didn't."

"Yes, you did. We saw you go into his office."

"But you couldn't have! You stayed behind in the car, listening to classical music, because you didn't want to get involved."

"We only pretended we didn't want to get involved," Bob said in his comforting bass. "This may come as a surprise, Abby, but we care about you. We can't sit by and watch you do something—uh—"

"Stupid?"

"Your word, Abby, not mine."

"Thanks a lot! And for your information, guys, Chisholm Banncock IX was not in his office this morning."

"But you came with C.J.'s pedigree."

"His secretary was a pushover. She had a vain streak a mile long. So, can we swing by the Banncock homestead? I figure we have just enough time before Greg gets home from shrimping."

"You know where Chiz lives?"

"No, but I'll call C.J. She's bound to know."

"I know where he lives," Rob said quietly.

That got Bob's attention. Mine too.

"How do you know?" I demanded.

"Because I delivered an exquisite, and very expensive, pair of early Lalique vases to him myself. Bob, you remember me mentioning a run out there, don't you?"

Bob grunted, and a bullfrog in a drainage ditch nearby answered.

"Well," I said, in an upbeat tone, "why don't we hustle our bustles back downtown so I can give the lad the third degree?"

Rob flushed. "He doesn't live downtown, Abby."

"Of course he does. He comes from an old Charleston family, doesn't he?"

Rob nodded, "Older than God, but they're not downtown—they're even better."

"Plantation people?"

"A rice plantation up near Awendaw, north of Mount Pleasant.

"What fun. I've always wanted to visit a rice plantation."

"Of course, it isn't a plantation now—hasn't been since the slaves were freed. In fact—and this I got straight from the horse's mouth—he plans to develop most of it into some kind of super golf-tennis community with deep water access. He's marketing it to folks from New Jersey. In fact, I think you have to be from New Jersey to buy a lot. But of course he's saved the nicest parcel for himself"

"*What?* Why, that hypocrite! He won't sell a downtown property to a native Southerner without a sterling pedigree, but he's chopping up the plantation and selling it to Yankees?"

"Abby, the lots with deep water access are going for more than a million dollars. You should see all the stretch limos driving up and down that dirt road."

I shook my head. "We can't possibly be talking about the same person. The Chisholm Banncock I know looks like a Greek god. He gets his nickname Chiz from his chiseled cheeks, not Chisholm. And did I mention he has dimples deep enough to hide olives in?"

"That's him—a real stocking stuffer, eh?"

"He could stuff my socks any day—" I slapped my own mouth. I was a happily married woman.

"So when were you going to tell me this?" Bob bellowed. The bullfrog in the drainage ditch was not to be outdone.

"Tell you what, dear?"

"Not you, Abby. Rob. When was he going to tell me about this Greek god named Chiz?"

I could see Rob's face muscles tense. "Robert," he said sharply, "get a grip on it, will you? The man is as straight as Highway 17. You don't think Abby would be drooling like a mastiff, would you, if he weren't?"

"Hey!" I cried. "I resent that remark."

"Give me a break, Abby. You're standing on your tongue."

"Can I help it if I'm short? Look guys, we better get a move on it. It's four o'clock already, and rush hour traffic is fierce in Mount Pleasant, what with all the retired New Jerseyites—and New Yorkers too— who still haven't gotten rush hour out of their blood."

"Yeah," Bob said, slipping into a better mood, "it's funny how they hit the road every day between four-thirty and six, even when they have no place to go."

"Home to Happy Hour?" Rob suggested.

We left it at that, and vamoosed before the traffic got worse.

The Mark Clark Expressway from North Charleston to Mount Pleasant passes over some spectacular bridges, and would be a pleasant ride were it not for the fumes from the paper plant sitting on the west bank of the Cooper River, and the constant threat of death from the myriad container trucks that rumble along at speeds meant for fighter-jet pilots. Between gasps— due to both the air and our narrow escapes—I contemplated life in the greater Charleston area.

One cannot find a more beautiful or hospitable city, but like an ice sculpture, the fragile beauty that gives Charleston County its charm might soon be its undoing. The bucolic Lowcountry scenery with its salt marshes dotted with hammocks of oak and pal-metto, draws perspective residents like jam bread draws flies. The ice sculpture is melting fast. Massive homes rim the marshes and there is heated debate on the wisdom of expanding Charleston's harbor, the fifth busiest in the nation. Most reasonable people see both sides of the issue, before coming down firmly on one side or the other. A larger harbor means an expanding economy, but a shrinking natural landscape. More people means a greater number of services—important ones like good shopping malls and theaters with stadium seating—but bumper-to-bumper rush hour traffic on Highway 17.

By taking Long Point Road we were able to skirt most of the traffic, although going back into Charleston, across the Grace Memorial Bridge, would be another story. One thing for sure, Rob had not been exaggerating about the dirt road, or the line of limos creeping back and forth along its two-mile length. Who knew the Garden State had so many prosperous refugees? But on closer inspection I noticed a good number bore New York and Connecticut plates, and I even spied some South Carolina plates. The last might well have been rentals hired by wealthy Californians fleeing rolling blackouts.

We veered suddenly from the main dirt road on to what was the original, colonial drive. The arching oaks formed a complete tunnel, and their trailing skirts of moss brushed the top of Rob's SUV. It was an enchanting world, one that recalled a world of carriages filled with fanning ladies and their attentive beaus—as long as one could block out the fact that this world was built by the forced labor of kidnapped Africans and their descendants. This fact was impossible to ignore, when between the swooping branches I spotted the first in a long line of slave cabins.

Rob informed us that these buildings—crumbling wooden huts, really—were original. So was the main house. If that was the case, it seemed doubtful that the Banncock family had done any repairs to their manor since the end of the Late Unpleasantness.

"I don't get it," I said. "How can someone who lives in a ruin buy valuable antiques?"

"You'll see," Rob said. The last time I saw a grin that wide was back in fifth grade, when Tommy Hollingsworth hid a lizard in my lunch box.

The lane split when it encountered a circular bed of overgrown boxwood and we followed the left branch to the back of the house. Suddenly Bob and I gasped, depriving the vehicle of its oxygen.

"Ah, so you see it," Rob said devilishly.

18

To tell you the truth, I wasn't quit sure what my bug eyes were seeing. My first impression was that the *National Enquirer* had been right all along. Aliens had indeed landed on earth and established a colony at the rear of Chiz Banncock's derelict rice plantation.

Reason, however, told me that I had already seen two structures similar to this one on nearby Sullivan's Island. The rounded "flying saucer" houses on Sullivan's Island were not inhabited by aliens—as far as I knew—and were given their odd shape to make them resistant to hurricane-force winds. They appeared to be single-family homes and made of concrete. Chiz's house was more like a flying saucer hotel, and appeared to be metal. It could accommodate the Jetsons, all their friends and relatives, and still have room for a couple of summer rental units. Unlike the houses on Sullivan's Island, which are a curiosity, Chisholm Banncock the IX's version was a monstrosity. I tried to blink it away.

"Is it still there?" I asked in desperation.

"I'm afraid so," Bob moaned. The bullfrog back in North Charleston moaned as well.

"It has ten bedrooms," Rob said, "and nineteen bathrooms, just like Bill Gates's house. Tell me, Abby, why the hell would somebody want that many bathrooms?"

"Beats me! That's at least nineteen toilets to scrub. Possibly a few bidets as well."

"You can bet this Chiz guy doesn't clean his own johns," Bob said. He poked Rob in the back. "How do you know he has ten bedrooms?"

Rob grimaced. "Because he told me—and no, I didn't see any of them. I just dropped off the vases and left."

Bob sniffed. "Well, you don't have to get so huffy."

We pulled to a stop in front of the behemoth saucer just in time. "Beam me up, Scotty," I cried, as I stepped out into the muggy late afternoon air.

Rob laughed. He seemed glad to have a reason.

"He has an elevator. Actually two of them."

"Where's the doorbell?"

"There." Rob pointed to a silver tube to the right of a short, flagstone path. A golf ball-size black button protruded from the end of the tube. "You press on that."

"Yes? What is it?"

I practically sailed out of my sandals. I hadn't seen the round speaker ball, which was partially embedded in the pine needles that covered the ground. When I'd pushed on the button, it rose from the soil on a tube of its own.

"Chiz—uh—Mr. Banncock, this is Abigail Washburn. We met at my friend Jane Cox's house the night of Madame Woo-Woo's séance."

"The séance?" He seemed as blank as a bevy of bottle blonds.

"I flirted shamelessly with you, remember?"

"Ah yes, the feisty one in the hoop skirt."

"The *young* feisty one in the hoop skirt. The other was my mama."

"What can I do for you, Mrs. Washburn?"

"I'd like to ask you a few questions, if you don't mind."

"Are you alone?"

Was that a trick question? Surely he was checking me out through a window—or was that a portal? I wouldn't be at all surprised if a periscope rose up in front of my face. For all I knew, he'd already managed to probe me without my knowledge. Maybe even taken a DNA sample.

"I have two friends with me," I yelled, although I'm sure my excess volume wasn't necessary. "Two *men* friends. In fact, one of them you've already met—the big and burly Rob Goldburg."

Rob beamed. Bob glowered.

"What am I, chopped liver?" he growled.

There followed a moment of silence. "Okay," the

voice from the speaker ball said. "Come on up and bring your friends. Use elevator two. It's on the left."

"Thanks. We'll be right there."

"Not me," Rob said.

"What?" I cried. "But you have to!"

"I'd rather wander around the grounds, Abby. Bob can go with you."

Bob mumbled something unintelligible. It was clearly meant to get Rob's goat.

I stamped my foot. "You will wander around these grounds together, damn it. And if—I mean *when*—I return, you'll have this worked out."

There wasn't an ice sculpture's chance in a Charleston summer that they'd have the problem resolved, and I knew it. The problem, as I saw it, was that Bob was insecure—both about his looks and his origins. His best feature is his voice. Physically, he's on the spindly side, with a disproportionately large head that was beginning to bald. Bob has admitted that, when he was a boy, neighborhood bullies would taunt him with the epithet "Monster Head."

As far as his origins go—well, there's nothing to be done about that either. Bob hails from Toledo, Ohio. I once caught him slurring the T word, hoping to make it sound like Tupelo, which is in Mississippi. When he says "daddy" it comes out in two syllables, instead of the proper three. Despite his claim to being a gourmet cook, he omits sugar from his iced tea, but puts it in his cornbread. Enough said.

The men trudged off, properly chastised, and I turned my attention back to the house from Mars.

It was a toss-up. My right eye couldn't help but look at Chiz's chiseled face, and since he was wearing a smoking jacket, with no shirt underneath, his chiseled chest as well. My left eye, meanwhile, strained to take in my bizarre surroundings.

The interior walls of the house were made of a substance that looked similar to that used on the outside shell. Much to my surprise the shiny silver backdrop was an effective foil for the traditional furnishings.

"You're wondering if I get hot, aren't you?"

I will admit to being startled, that's all. "I *beg* your pardon?"

Chiz's dimples deepened. "I meant the ambient temperature in here. The answer, by the way, is no. The exterior is made from a new kind of highly reflective steel that actually repels ninety-nine percent of the sun's rays. It's the winter temperatures I have to worry about, but I have a kick-ass furnace, and I figure what I spend in winter heating, I save on summer cooling. As for the interior walls—well, they're actually just ordinary wallboard covered with industrial grade aluminum foil."

I took my right eye off the chiseled chest to better admire the odd choice of wallpaper. In the unlikely event the house caught on fire, Chiz would bake like a nice Idaho potato.

"This really is fascinating," I said.

"Would you like the full tour?"

I recoiled, as if he'd asked if I'd like the Full Monty. Yes, I know, I'm happily married, but my libido is alive and well, and occasionally requires a little extra effort to keep it in check.

"Some other time, maybe. For now I've got a ton of questions I need to ask—uh, if you're amenable."

"Ask away." He smiled and pointed to a wing armchair with floral upholstery. Made in Boston, probably in the seventeen hundreds, there was nothing space age about it.

I took the proffered seat, while he took a matching one. "Mr. Banncock—"

"Please, call me Chiz. Folks who share a murder should be on a first-name basis, right?"

"Right. And you call me Abby." I paused to reflect on what he'd said, which was surprisingly difficult given all the foil. "Uh—just to clarify something, Chiz. We didn't share a murder."

He laughed. "I guess that came out wrong. So, Abby, what would you like to know?"

"Well, for starters, did you happen to see anyone in the dining room—alone—before the séance that night?"

He cocked his head to think. "No, can't say that I did. But there was good food in the kitchen and pretty ladies—so I can't say that I paid the dining room a whole lot of attention. Not before the séance, at any rate."

"Okay. Now my second question is a little more personal."

"Eight inches," he said deadpan.

"*What?*"

"Eight inches. That's all the insulation I need between the steel shell and the interior framework."

"Oh!" I took a deep breath. "It isn't about insulation, I'm afraid. It's about Golda Feinstein—AKA Madame Woo-Woo."

The chiseled features darkened. It was like the sun setting on Mount Rushmore.

"I don't discuss my love life with folks I hardly know."

"But you did have one—with her, I mean?"

He jumped to his feet. "Abby, I'm afraid your interview is over."

"I'm sorry you feel that way. I just want to help."

"Who says I need help?"

"Well, if I was able to get ahold of this interesting bit of information, you can bet the police have as well. Hmm, let's see . . . wealthy, well-connected boyfriend dumps girlfriend who demands too much. She has something on him, so he does her in."

"I didn't kill Golda!"

"Maybe you didn't, but you have to admit that you being there that night looks mighty strange. You were the only one there, besides C.J., who wasn't a Heavenly Hooker—I mean, Hustler!"

"What about you?"

"My mama's a Hooker—I mean, Hustler! I was helping her with the food. Besides, I don't have a motive."

"I bet I could find one, if you gave me a minute."

"Go for it."

He sat back on the upholstered chair. "There are those Portuguese tiles in the kitchen."

"So?"

"So, they're extremely valuable, aren't they?"

"Are they?"

"Abby, I'm not playing games now. You were drooling over those tiles the night of Golda's murder."

"So?" That little S word was really quite useful. I picked up its finer nuances when my kids were combative teenagers.

"I'm suggesting that Golda's murder might have been a decoy."

"A decoy?"

"I know this house doesn't have any echoes, so you must be hard of hearing. Allow me to repeat myself. You used Golda's murder as a decoy. You knew the house was being renovated—perhaps even helped with the renovations—learned about the tiles, and then had to figure some way to distract folks while you pondered what to do with them."

"That's the stupidest thing I ever heard. Those tiles

were worth about three hundred dollars apiece. Maybe four, for the better ones. Let's say there were a hundred of them—well, you do the math. Do I look like I need three or four thousand dollars enough to murder someone for it?"

"I just did the math, Abby. It comes to thirty thousand, not three. And that was a long wall. I bet there were at least two hundred tiles on it, which would bring the total to—"

"I know!" I wailed. "Sixty thousand dollars. I've always been dismal at math."

"Abby, if that wall was a complete panel—say from some important castle or palace, how much would it be worth? As a whole?"

My mind flashed to an article I'd read about a retired English couple who bought a modest home in the south of Spain, but alas, too far inland to catch the sea breezes. They removed the worn wall-to-wall carpet only to find the floor consisted of early Spanish tiles worth a tidy half million U.S. dollars. They sold the entire house to a tile collector and bought a villa on a cliff overlooking the Mediterranean.

"Well," I said, "a whole lot more than three thousand, that's for sure."

He laughed politely. "Yes, but how much?"

"This is just a wild guess, mind you—but perhaps in the neighborhood of a quarter million."

"And what if there's something more than tiles hidden in those walls?"

My mouth fell open wide enough, I'm sure, to swallow a Spanish villa. "Who told you about the body in the wall?"

It was his turn to experience a sprained jaw. "Body? Did you say there was a body in the wall?"

I can't tell if a man means it when he says I'm not fat, or that the roast wasn't tough, but it didn't take a relationship maven to see that Chisholm Banncock IX was genuinely surprised by the revelation. Now that the cat—make that body—was out of the bag, I didn't see that I had anything to lose by filling him in on the details. And since he'd been the real estate agent, he might even be able to shed some light on the grisly matter.

Chiz listened as raptly as if he'd bought a dozen lottery tickets and the winning number was being read. His eyes were closed, and periodically a dimple would twitch. When I was through he opened his eyes halfway and regarded me under lashes so long they looked artificial.

"Jane Cox isn't planning to sue, is she?" he asked.

I must say, I hadn't thought of that. If a woman can sue a fast food restaurant just because she found a chicken beak in with her nuggets, then surely a home-owner can sue a real estate agent for selling her a house with a skeleton in the wall.

"I don't know what C.J. plans," I said, choosing my words carefully.

"But I didn't know the body was there. I swear."

"Maybe. But you knew the house was haunted, didn't you?"

I could see him relax. "That one I'm guilty of. I hadn't ever seen the ghost, or heard it, but everyone in Charleston—well, we natives at any rate—know about the ghost of Sarah MacGregor."

"So that really was her name?"

He nodded. "According to the story, she had a— uh—let's call it a romantic involvement with the house slave, a light-skinned mulatto named Henry. Her father found them together and killed the slave. Sarah was packed off to a boarding school up North. From there the story gets a little fuzzy. One version has her running away from boarding school with a professional gambler; another has her hitching a ride on a wagon train out West somewhere where she became a prostitute. At any rate, she was never seen again, never returned to Charleston—that is, until she died. One night her ghost showed up and started haunting the house, presumably looking for Henry."

"That's it!" I cried. And believe me, that weird house does have echoes.

"What's it?"

"The body in the wall—that was Sarah MacGregor. She never went up North. Her father killed her!"

I could see the light bulb go on in his head as well. It shone right through his dimples.

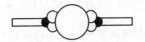

19

"You may be right," he said. "Assuming one believes in ghosts, of course."

"They prefer the term Apparition Americans. But there's one thing wrong with this theory—wait, did you tell Golda Feinstein about Sarah MacGregor?"

"Guilty again."

"As I was about to say, Madame Woo-Woo—I mean Golda—had Sarah MacGregor claim to be the mistress of the house. The Sarah in your story wasn't; she was the daughter."

"Ah. I guess I forgot to mention that the real Sarah MacGregor's mother died during childbirth. Apparently the baby was turned around—what do you call that?"

"Breech," I said.

"Yeah, that's it.

"Too bad we don't have fingerprints or DNA samples to compare the corpse with."

He grinned. "The doctor made a mess of things and

little Sarah was born with a finger missing."

"And that's somehow funny?"

He looked surprised. "No, but there's your physical evidence. If the skeleton you found in the wall is missing a finger, it's her."

"You may have something there." I gasped as I noticed the time on a grandfather clock that, somehow, didn't look out of place against a shiny silver wall. If there were no accidents on Highway 17, and if I took Mathis Ferry Road when I got to it, I just might beat Greg home.

"Is something wrong, Abby?"

"Time seems to have gotten away from me again, that's all." I hopped to my feet. "Mind if I ask you one last question?"

"Shoot."

"If I came into your downtown office tomorrow morning and asked to see a house, would you show it to me?"

"But Abby, Jane Cox is your friend. You'll have to work that out with her."

"No, I mean some *other* house. As a customer."

A true Southern gentleman, he'd stood when I did, and now he towered over me. "You want an honest answer?"

"I always want honest answers—unless they have to do with the way I look."

"Then the answer is no."

"Because I'm from off? Because I'm not a blue blood?"

"In a word, yes."

"But that's illegal! That's discrimination!"

"Of course it is. But as with everything, there are ways to get around the law."

"*How* would you do it?"

He glanced around, as if he was nervous. Perhaps the metal sphere had ears.

"I'd stonewall you. For starters, I wouldn't return your calls—most folks from off can't stand that. If you showed up at the office, my secretary would tell you I wasn't in."

"What if I caught you in the office?"

"Well, then I'd have to help, legally, but I'd be late for showing appointments, or conveniently forget them altogether. If you persisted—demanded my cooperation—I'd show you a few houses, but you wouldn't like them. Not when I got done with my spiel."

"But *why*? Isn't 'off' money as good as 'on' money?"

He smiled. "Of course it is. And there are plenty of other real estate agents who would be happy to take it. It's just that I, for one, prefer to work with the older, more established clientele."

"Then you're a hypocrite, because that dirt road out there is clogged with the Sopranos."

"Come again?"

"Okay, so maybe they're not all from New Jersey, but they are from so far off, they're practically on again."

Chisholm Banncock IX groaned. For a split second I thought maybe he had appendicitis. It can come on real fast, you know. It happened to Buford, who had to be rushed to the hospital within an hour of the first pain. The doctors said his appendix was as hot as a Tijuana tamale, and could burst at any moment. Within minutes he was on the operating table. Unfortunately, he recovered.

"Are you all right, dear?"

"Yeah, if you can call it that. You see, that property isn't mine—not anymore. I sold it to a cousin, who promised to keep it in the family. But the pull of Yankee dollars was just too strong. All I own is the little patch of ground around this house."

"You don't even own the main house? Or the slave cabins?"

"I'm afraid not. But I guess things could be worse. A group of musicians from Newark bought the house. They plan to renovate it themselves and turn it into a retirement home for oboe and clarinet players. Gone With the Winds they're going to call it."

I thanked Chiz for his time and took the elevator back down to reality. The Rob-Bobs were back at the car, looking much happier.

*   *   *

We crept across the Grace Memorial Bridge in record time. That is to say, it took longer than I can ever remember it taking, thanks to a car that ran out of gas midway and had to be pushed because there was no room to get a tow truck near it. Perhaps it is age, perhaps just maturity, but at times like these I find that the Zen approach is the only way to go. While Rob pounded the steering wheel and Bob invented naughty limericks about other antique dealers we all knew and loathed, I enjoyed the scenery. Charleston harbor is one of the prettiest sights in the world, and I had a bird's-eye view.

Unfortunately, my petite progenitress has never experienced a Zen moment in her life, and might never do so, even after she's dead. When the Rob-Bobs dropped me off, with admonitions to be good and stay out of trouble, Mama met me at the door with her hands on her hips. She looked like a mother hen whose only chick had decided to go for a swim in the farm pond.

"Abby, where have you been?"

"Hanging out with my friends, Mama."

"Abby, there were reporters here. I had to deal with them all by myself."

"Reporters? From what? *The Post & Courier?*"

"That, and the local network stations. They wanted details about you finding a body in C.J.'s house. Abby, is that really true? Did you find a body?"

"Oh, Mama, it was awful!"

She did the motherly thing and clasped me briefly to her bosom, taking care all the while not to crush her crinolines. Sometimes I forget she was my very first friend.

"Did it smell?" she asked, fluffing up her skirt.

"What?"

"The body. You know I have an incredible nose, dear." She couldn't help but smile proudly.

"Yes, Mama, you claim to have the best sniffer in the entire South. You claim you can actually smell trouble coming. Well, you didn't this time, did you?"

The worried hen look returned. "Abby, do you think I should see a doctor? I mean, there I was, not a foot away from the wall the night of the séance, and I didn't smell a thing."

I wandered into the living room and hoisted myself into a chair. It had been an incredibly long day and my dogs were barking. Mama, as I knew she would, followed and took a chair of her own. And speaking of smells, the aroma of her post roast drifted pleasantly into the room from the kitchen.

"Mama, you couldn't smell anything, until you actually broke through the wallboard. Then it was awful. But please, I'd rather talk about something else."

"Afraid it will spoil your dinner, dear?"

"No. What I want to talk about is the work you and the Heavenly Hustlers were doing for C.J.—without her knowledge!"

Mama didn't smell that one coming, although she

did recoil like she'd just gotten a whiff of bad fish. She popped to her feet.

"No time to talk now, Abby. Your hubby will be home any minute, and I haven't even started on the potatoes."

"Make noodles, Mama. They take less time. We need to talk—and before Greg gets home."

"Abby, you're not going to yell at me, are you?"

Now, how do you suppose that makes a good daughter feel? I wouldn't dream of yelling at the woman who'd endured thirty-six hours of excruciating pain on my behalf. Not when sarcasm is a much more effective tool.

"Why should I yell, Mama? I'm not in the least bit vexed."

"You're *not?*"

"Not in the least. It wasn't me who thought she had a remodeling ghost on her hands. It will be interesting, however, to see how C.J. reacts when she gets here. She's still staying with us, right?"

Mama nodded. The hen had no idea what her chick would do next. Maybe it would even walk on water.

"Do we have to tell C.J., dear? It was meant to be a surprise—a good surprise."

"Yes, we have to tell her. The police are going to tell her anyway. In fact, they probably already have."

Mama squirmed. "C.J.'s a sweetheart, Abby. You know she is. She's not likely to do anything—uh, dangerous, is she?"

"Mama, she's one of your best friends. How can you even suggest that? Just because her cousin, Orville Ledbettter, attacked six people with a Ping-Pong paddle on a cruise ship, because one of them stepped on his ball, doesn't mean our C.J. will react violently. And that story about her Aunt Lavinia believing she was a condor and jumping off Half Dome in Yosemite National Park simply isn't true. She did not, as C.J. claims, fly a hundred feet before falling, and as a result break every bone in her body except her nose. Lavinia jumped off a much lower cliff, and she landed in a pine tree. A broken wrist was the extent of her injuries."

Mama sighed with relief. "I didn't think she'd go bonkers, Abby. But with those folks from Shelby, you can never be sure."

"Yeah, well, one thing for sure is that it was a member of your Heavenly Hustlers club who killed Madame Woo-Woo, AKA Golda Feinstein."

Mama blanched. "Oh, Abby, that's just so hard to believe. They're all such nice, normal people."

For some reason the intergalactic bar scene in the first *Star Wars* movie popped into mind. If those creatures could be considered normal, then maybe the Hustlers stood a chance.

"Mama, no matter how nice they seem to you, one of them is a killer. You have to stop associating with all of them."

Except for the day of Daddy's death, and the funeral, I have never known Mama to cry. She seemed on the verge of tears now.

"If you think it's best, dear. But I'm going to be very lonely."

"But you needn't be, Mama. There are oodles of opportunities for you to volunteer at church."

"I know that, dear, but I want to kick up my heels—have a little fun."

"Well, volunteer in the church office during the week, but on Saturdays go skydiving."

Mama's shimmering tears dried as fast as dew in a Carolina August, and her trembling lips transformed into a smile. "That's a wonderful idea, dear. I'll look up skydiving companies in the Yellow Pages right after supper."

If I'd been wearing pointy pumps, instead of summer sandals, I would have gladly kicked myself. Mama wasn't bluffing. At least if neither the main nor the spare chute opened, her voluminous skirt and its requisite petticoats might slow her descent a little. Still, I had to try and stop her.

"You might not be as lucky as C.J.'s Aunt Lavinia. Things could go terribly wrong and you might live to tell the story—only your mouth could be on the back of your head. It wouldn't be a pretty sight."

"Charleston has plenty of good plastic surgeons," she said, not in the least bit discouraged.

"You'll probably have to wear some sort of unfashionable jumpsuit. Otherwise folks in both London and France might see your underpants."

Mama flung her skirt over her head, but mercifully, after a few seconds, yanked it down. "Abby, at my age, modesty means nothing."

I suppose that's why she survived a week in a nudist camp three years ago. Granted, it was a ladies only nudist camp, and then, only for ladies of "a certain age." The brochure described it as "a retreat for ladies of breeding who want to experience the world as God had originally intended them to." I was never quite sure if it was a religious cult, but when Mama returned she was still an Episcopalian, and wasn't into hugging trees or kissing toads. She'd had a lovely time—except for when she'd inadvertently sat on a hot metal stair. She claimed that since she'd been allowed to keep her pearls on, she hadn't even felt naked. Her pearls! They were the solution.

"Suppose," I said wickedly, "the string in your pearls breaks. I know, they're knotted individually, but the entire necklace could come off. You would almost certainly never see it again."

My progenitress's petite paws flew to her throat. "Perish the thought, Abby! You don't think that could really happen, do you?"

"Most certainly. You and your pearls are bound to fall at separate rates. Why, they could land a mile away—maybe in a pond or something. Say sayonara to your Mikimotos."

"Then skydiving is definitely out. I guess I'm just destined to be a lonely old widow." The tears threatened to spill again.

"I saw the strangest house today," I said to divert her attention. "It looked like a flying saucer."

"Chiz Banncock's house," Mama sniffed.

"You've seen it?"

"Of course, dear. Remember that cocktail party I attended last month?"

"That was in the space ship?"

Mama rolled her eyes. At least they were dry again. "Sometimes I think you don't listen to a word I say. I told you all about it at supper that night. Remember I said we were all there, except for Hugh, because he and Sondra were having a bit of a tiff? Frankly, Abby, I don't think their marriage is long for the books."

"That's nice, Mama. And while we're on the subject of Chisel Cheeks IX, you need to stay away from him too. He was there on the night of Golda Feinstein's murder."

"But he's just a boy!"

"He's in his thirties, I'll bet. That's no boy."

Mama twirled her precious pearls in agitation. "Well, I guess the tables have finally turned, haven't they, dear?"

"I beg your pardon?"

"When you were little, I tried to pick your friends. And now you're trying to pick mine."

"My friends pushed beans up their noses, Mama. They didn't kill each other."

"Thelma Maypole would never kill anyone. I was out to her house on Kiawah Island one day when a palmetto bug ran across the kitchen floor. This was a really big roach, Abby. If I could have found a saddle to fit, I could have ridden him back into town. Anyway, Thelma cornered him, managed to scoop him into a paper cup, and took him outside. Can you guess what she did then?"

"Changed into old shoes and did the tarantella on top of the bugger?"

"No. She released him. Now, would a woman who released a cockroach outside be capable of killing another woman?"

"Himmler loved dogs," I said. "Mama, speaking of Thelma—she told me that she mentioned to you seeing Dr. Whipperspoonbill alone in the dining room before the séance. Is that true?"

"Did she? Abby, my mind is all a blur, what with bodies turning up left and right. But don't think for a minute that Francis is Madame Woo-Woo's killer. We took a trip to Mintken Abbey once, and we got caught in a frog-strangler of a rain. Francis loaned me his umbrella. I don't mean he just shared it, dear—we couldn't both fit under it and keep my skirt dry. The dear man walked around without a thought for his clothes or hair."

"The dear man is bald, Mama."

"Yes, well—"

The front door opened, and the love of my life stepped in. One look at his face and I wanted to drive straight up to Mintken Abbey and hide out in a monk's cell.

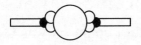

20

Fortunately, the first thing my sweetheart does when he comes home is take a long, hot shower. This is not a luxury, mind you, but a necessity. The only living being that will get close to him, sans shower, is my cat Dmitri. If I've neglected to mention the smallest male in my life, I apologize. You see what stress can do to a gal? At any rate, Dmitri runs to welcome Greg, rubs against his legs, licks his shoes, and begs to be picked up. That is because my beloved enters the house smelling like the Mount Pleasant fish market on a summer day without electricity.

With Greg soaping down, and Dmitri rolling about in his discarded clothes, I fixed myself a stiff drink (an entire jigger!) of rum and Diet Coke, and worked on a string of rebuttals. Actually, it wasn't that hard. Yes, dear. I'm sorry, dear. I'll never do it again, dear. Those have all worked very well in the past. Because I'm a cheap date, likely to fall asleep on just half a beer, the rum in the coke was to get me properly subdued. What I didn't count on was C.J. coming home quite so early.

"Ooh, Abby," she said, catching her breath when she saw me drink in hand, "they're not sending you up the river, are they?"

"Excuse me?"

"I heard all about you clobbering that cop. One of your customers today—I think it was Angela Duckworth—said you could get twenty years for that. But if they're just sending you up the river—well, that's not so bad. Cousin Alvin Ledbetter got sent up the river, and discovered the headwaters of the Nile."

There was no need to offer C.J. a drink. The big gal may be extremely bright, but she has a perpetual happy hour going on in her head.

"John Hanning Speke was the first European to correctly identify Lake Victoria as a source of the Nile. But no, C.J., nobody's sending me anywhere."

She looked at me, her face shining with admiration. "Wow! You talked yourself out of another tight one, didn't you, Abby?"

I shrugged modestly. "Well, the woman was being a jerk. You can't desecrate a corpse like that—" I stopped. Mama only rarely cried, C.J. never did—until now. Tears the size of olives were plopping on my antique carpet. I don't mean to sound petty, but that was a lot of salt for those ancient wool fibers to contend with.

"Ooh, Abby," she said, and then threw herself into

my arms. A word to the wise; if you're four-nine and a five feet, ten inch big-boned woman hurls herself at you, either duck, or brace yourself. I did neither, and C.J. and I found ourselves crammed into the same armchair, with me on the bottom. My drink, of course, went everywhere.

I used some impolite words while extricating myself, but I wasn't angry with C.J. "It's got to be damned hard having a body found behind your fridge," I said.

"Ooh, Abby, you don't know the half of it. How am I supposed to ever sleep in that house again? I mean, what if there are more of them? There could even be one in the floor under my bed."

I gulped the remains of my drink, which seemed to have become as necessary as Greg's shower. "C.J., I don't think there are any more. I think this is the only one. But since you asked, I'd make Chisholm Banncock IX buy that house back from you. If he refuses, I'd sue his butt from here to Timbuktu. Then I'd buy a nice *new* house. Over in Mount Pleasant they're building what looks like a replica of Colonial Lake. It's called I'On. The houses are all new—no one has died in them yet."

She nodded. "Can I stay here, with you, until I find a new place?"

What do you say when your best friend asks to move in with you under dire circumstances? That's like having to choose between a drought or three feet of rain all at once. At least with C.J around—she would be the rain—Greg would be forced to display company manners. Not that he mistreats me, mind you, but you know what I mean. After all, my informal investigation was bound to get thornier before it was over.

"Sure," I said, "be our guest—but try not to sleep on your back. Last night you sounded like a force five hurricane. Even Greg woke up. Don't tell him I told you, but he was shouting 'evacuate, evacuate!' "

C.J. giggled and then lunged at me again. "Ooh, you're the very best friend a girl could have."

I'd managed to dodge her clumsy affection and remain upright. "Well, I'm not a diamond."

"Yes, you are! You're a diamond, and a pearl, and a black rooster's knuckles."

"What the heck kind of combination is that?"

"That's a good luck charm, Abby. Everybody knows that. Granny Ledbettter sells oodles of them in Shelby. Of course the diamonds are very small, on account of them being so expensive."

I grabbed one of her sturdy wrists and steered her to a chair. Then I gave her a gentle shove to make her sit.

"C.J., we need to talk."

"Sure, Abby. I wasn't planning on doing anything this evening except roll my hair and conjugate Chinese verbs." She was serious on both counts. I don't know if curling irons have made it to Shelby, but C.J.

rolls her dishwater blond hair every night on orange juice cans. And as for the Chinese verbs, the same girl who is two ants shy of a picnic speaks seventeen languages.

"We need to talk *now*, C.J. Before Greg gets out of the shower."

"Don't be silly, Abby. I've already had that talk."

"You have? But—"

"Granny Ledbetter told me where babies come from."

I resolved to ask her, on another occasion, and with a full beer in hand, what her Granny had to say on the subject. "C.J., sugar, what I want to talk to you about is your house. You know that remodeling you thought was being done by a ghost—er, Apparition American? Well, it wasn't. Mama and her friends were sneaking into your house."

C.J., who should have been spitting mad, was beaming. "Mozella is such a sweet friend—and so are you, Abby. And now I have all these other new friends too."

"If you mean the Heavenly Hustlers, forget it. One of them is a murderer, remember?"

My pal processed that. "Ooh, Abby, you're right. I've always been too trusting, I guess. When I was younger I'd go home with any adult who claimed to be my parent."

"Little kids sometimes do that."

"I was in high school, Abby."

"C.J., dear, please focus. I want to ask you about that wall in your kitchen. You have an incredible mind for antiques. Didn't you have the slightest idea it was covered with precious tiles?"

She shook her big shaggy head. "They were all painted, Abby—you saw that—except for the ones behind the fridge, which came with the house. Ooh, Abby, I know what you're thinking. You think I'm dirty because I don't clean the dust bunnies out from behind there."

"I was thinking no such thing." The truth be known, I never clean behind my refrigerator, unless I'm replacing it—or selling a house. But that was it! That was the one question I'd forgotten to ask Chiz. Who owned the house before C.J. bought it? On the off chance she might know, I posed the question to my friend.

"Ooh, Abby, don't you remember anything?"

"Of course I do!"

"Sometimes I don't think you do, Abby. Otherwise you would have remembered it was that chubby woman with the funny glasses. Selma, I think her name is."

Then it hit me like a ton of C.J.s. "Thelma Maypole?"

"Yeah, but you sure the first name isn't Selma?"

"Positive. C.J., are we talking about the same stout woman who was at the séance?"

"Yeah." She bit her lip. "Ooh, Abby, I hope she wasn't offended by all the changes your Mama's friends made."

"C.J., tell me about the changes."

"Well, there was this really good fake Tiffany lampshade in the downstairs powder room—"

"The one you have a scarf draped over now?"

"Yeah, I'd been meaning to go to Home Depot to get me a new one—lamp, I mean. One with less green in it. Now, where was I, Abby?"

"You were telling me about all the changes the Heavenly Hustlers made, and you started with the lamp in the downstairs powder room."

"Yeah, well, Mozella's friends got me a new one from Home Depot, just like I wanted. But it still has too much green in it to suit my taste. Abby, do you think I should say anything?"

"Not just yet. What other changes can you think of?"

"Well, they stripped and sanded the banister. And let me tell you, Abby, it really needed it. Oh, and they put in all new screens."

"That's nice, dear, but what about decorative details? Anything else along the lines of replacing the Tiffany-style lamp?"

She scratched her head. "Well, there's the downstairs bathroom again. Miss Maypole had these big old ugly gold handles on the faucets. Abby, I can't tell you how happy I was when the ghost—I mean, your

mama's friends—replaced those right fast with some
nice plastic ones. Too bad they didn't get around to
replacing the ones upstairs."

"You're kidding, right?"

"Abby, you know I love antiques, and my living
room is full of them, but the bathroom is for personal
business. Why, on Granny Ledbetter's farm we didn't
even have a bathroom."

"You had an outhouse, I presume."

"Actually, we didn't. But we did each have our
own little patch of corn. The only problem was in the
winter, after they cut the corn down."

"Spare me the details!" I shook my head to clear it
of the images that had already started to creep in.
"C.J., do you mind if I check a few things out at your
house?"

"Abby, I'm sure I turned off the gas. Granny taught
me to hop three times on my left, turn off the gas, and
then hop three times on the right. Of course you have
to sing a little song while you do it. See, so even if
you forget whether or not you've turned off the gas,
you still remember hopping and singing."

"That's nice, dear, but I'm not worried about
whether or not you left your stove on. I want your
permission to poke around a bit."

"Okey-dokey, Abby, but please don't poke into
more walls. I couldn't stand it if you found another
body."

"Don't worry—"

Mama poked her head in the door. "Supper is in five minutes."

She must have gone with the noodles. At any rate, no sooner did she step back into the kitchen then Greg emerged from our bedroom freshly scrubbed. Dmitri trailed behind him, trying to get a sniff of his cuffs.

"Hey, C.J.," Greg said, and gave her a polite peck on the cheek. It would have been horrible Southern manners for him not to have done so, but I think he is genuinely fond of the girl. I get the impression he views her as the sister he never had.

C.J. giggled. "You smell like bouillabaisse."

Greg laughed. "I'll take that as a compliment." He turned to me. "Sweetheart, care to take a walk before supper?"

That was the moment of reckoning. Fortunately, I had a legitimate excuse to postpone it.

"Mama just gave us the five-minute warning."

Greg winked at C.J. "We'll be less than five minutes," I promise.

"But she's making noodles. You know how they clump together if they're not served right away."

Greg took my right hand in both of his and pulled me gently to the front door. "But I haven't had a chance to eat my last meal," I wailed.

"You will."

I could hear the beat of the death drums. I didn't have a snowball's chance in Charleston of escaping lecture number three hundred and twenty-four. The only thing to do was to square my shoulders and take it like a woman.

Greg ushered me outside, but stopped on the porch. He leaned over, gave me a long, tight hug, and then a lingering kiss. He had just shaved, so I didn't have whisker burn to worry about. I returned his ardor. If I had to miss out on my final meal, a final kiss would have to do.

"Abby," he said, finally pushing me away, "please listen to what I'm going to say."

I caved. "Sure thing, sweetie, but just let me get this in first. I'm terribly sorry and I'll never do it again. I swear on a stack of Bibles taller than St. Michael's steeple. I'll be the perfect, adoring little wife you always wanted—just don't yell at me."

"Abby, I don't yell at you."

"Well, lecture then—it's the same thing."

Greg laughed and kissed me on the forehead. "Damn, you cheat me out of all my fun."

"You mean you won't lecture?"

"I was just going to tell you how proud I am of you."

"You *were*?"

"You betcha. You're feisty, Abby. I've always loved that about you."

"Yes, but I hit a woman. Even I know that's wrong."

"Abby, I'm not supposed to tell you this, but a certain detective, who shall remain nameless, says that woman deserved the punch you threw."

"Greg, she was a policewoman in uniform!"

"She was a jerk. And I'm not advocating you go around solving problems with those fists of yours, Abby—but some people just have it coming to them."

You could have knocked me over with a feather. "Come again?"

"You know, of course, I don't approve of your— dare I say meddling? But hell, I know I can't stop you. As my Daddy used to say, when you go to a mule's funeral, weep at the front end."

"What is that supposed to mean?"

He shrugged. "Beats me, but I've been waiting forty years to say it. I think it means you should know what you're dealing with, so you don't get any nasty surprises. I know I'm not going to make you toe the line, so I'm not going to kid myself."

"Hmm." I was still stuck on the mule metaphor.

Greg kissed me again. "We squared away then?"

I returned his kiss. "You betcha. But, darling, since it turns out you're not mad at me—would you mind doing me one teensy-weensy favor?"

He groaned good-naturedly. "Not another foot rub."

"Well, I certainly would not say no to one of those. But what I really want is for you to call Sergeant Scrubb and find out if Golda Feinstein—you know, Madame Woo-Woo—was pregnant. I told her brother to call and ask the same thing, but they might not tell him. At least not just yet."

"Will do."

"And one more thing. Would you please suggest that he have that corpse I found in the wall examined as well to see if it—I should say Sarah MacGregor—was pregnant? An autopsy should show that, shouldn't it?"

"I would think so—depending on how far along she was. Abby, where is this coming from?"

"Something a proud member of one of Charleston's oldest families told me. I'm trying to piece together the history of C.J.'s ghost. Oh, and I need to find out if she's missing a finger."

I got a third kiss. "You amaze me, Abby. You know that?"

"That's my intent. Keep the men in your life amazed, I always say."

"But hon, you've got to promise me you'll back out of any situation that looks dangerous."

I wanted to say "yeah, yeah, been there, promised that," but of course I didn't. I'm not *that* big of a fool. I promised to be as cautious as a long-tailed cat on a porch full of rockers. Then I coaxed him off our porch, which contained three rockers, and into the house to eat Mama's pot roast and noodles.

The noodles were delicious, by the way.

I slept far better than a baby that night; I slept like a teenager. When I awoke Greg and C.J. had both gone to work, and Mama was washing breakfast dishes. I rushed through my ablutions and grabbed a bagel before Mama put them away. Even though, in theory, we share the kitchen, and in fact, I own it, Mama rules it with an iron fist.

"Well, well, if it isn't sleepyhead," Mama said.

I yawned. "You got that right."

"Frankly, dear, I'm surprised to see you. After what I heard last night—I expected you to be in bed all day."

"Heard?"

Mama waggled her scant eyebrows. "You know."

"I'm afraid I don't." I wasn't being coy; I really didn't.

"Abby, there's no point in pretending with me. I know all about it. How do you think you got here? Although frankly, I haven't heard such carrying on since the time your daddy and I broke the bed at your Aunt Marilyn's house."

Then it dawned on me what she meant. I clapped the bagel over one ear, my free hand over the other.

"Mama, I don't want to hear another word."

She said a few more undoubtedly provocative things while I sang "Pop Goes the Weasel" at the top of my lungs. The second her lips stopped moving I got straight to business.

"Just for that you're coming with me to C.J.'s."

"I am? Whatever for, dear?"

She had that flight or fight look in her eyes, so I

stepped back into the doorway. "There are a few things I need to check out, Mama, and I'm not going back into that house alone."

"Well, don't expect me to come with you, dear. Just the thought of that woman, stuffed in the wall, gives me the shivers." To prove her point, Mama shimmied and shook like a drunken belly dancer. "Besides," she said, catching her breath, "what would Greg say?"

"My darling husband has given me his tacit approval."

"He said you could meddle?"

"He said he knew he couldn't stop me, so he warned me to be careful."

"Well, he can stop me. I have no intention of going."

"Mama, you owe me."

"What did you say, dear?" Mama had her hands on her hips, framing her still tiny waist. The thirty-six hours of agonizing labor was written all over her face, but at least I hadn't ruined her figure.

"Okay, so maybe you don't owe *me*, but you owe it to C.J. None of this would have happened—the stolen tiles, the body discovered in the wall—if it hadn't been for *your* meddling."

Mama grabbed her pearls and gave them a good hard spin. She was nailed to the wall, and she knew it. Of course, Mama is as stubborn as a blue-nosed mule, and had to get the last lick in.

"I suppose this is the thanks I get for all the sacrifices I've made."

"No, *this* is the thanks." I gave her a loud smooch on the cheek. "Please get ready, Mama. Time's a'wasting."

Mama got ready by untying her lace-edged, heart-shaped apron and turning her pearls so that the clasp was in back. Her sleuthing outfit was what she always wore; a nineteen fifties dress with a pinched waist and full circle skirt fluffed out by yards of starched crinoline. Her stockings had seams in the back, and her high-heel pumps tapered to points, and could be used as ice picks in an emergency. In other words, I was taking Donna Reed with me on this follow-up investigation.

In contrast I was wearing knee-length white shorts, a silk blend T-shirt, and white strap sandals. This was barely acceptable summer attire for year-round-residents. Only a hooch or a tourist would wear a halter top in Charleston.

Although I'd brought my key with me, I made Mama open the door with her key. She protested at first that she didn't have one, but sure enough, there it was inside the handbag that matched her shoes. The key was knotted in a handkerchief embroidered with violets.

The second she opened the door, the sweet musty smell of death assaulted our nostrils. "Abby," Mama cried, "I'm not going in there!"

"Put the handkerchief over your nose and mouth, Mama. It's just an old smell, one that's been bottled up in the wall for a hundred and fifty years."

"But, Abby, it smells like a mausoleum."

I had no time to ask her how she knew what a mausoleum smelled like, and it was clear she wasn't going to be much help if I ever got her inside. Fortunately C.J. has a nice shady patio. Like most of the city's gardens, it is small, but big on charm. The brick walls are traced with creeping fig and Confederate Jasmine. The miniature planting beds were chock-full of ginger, fatsia, and cast iron plants. A lion's head fountain hung on one wall and there were two wrought iron chairs and a round iron table in the middle of the space. An exceptionally handsome loquat tree presided over the scene.

"Mama, hang out in the garden while I go in. But keep your ears open, just in case I scream."

Mama clutched her pearls. "Abby, is there something you're not telling me? Do you think someone's hiding in there?"

"No, Mama. I said, 'just in case.' I'll be fine. Honest. But—and this is another 'just in case' scenario—if I'm not out in twenty minutes, go next door and call Greg." I could slap myself for not having remembered to bring my cell phone.

She nodded. "I'll be praying for you, Abby."

I was touched by her offer, but not altogether comforted. The only prayer I've heard Mama say aloud, other than the ones in the Book of Common Prayer, is her daily plea that my brother, Toy, will get married before his fortieth birthday.

I left Mama clutching her pearls and mouthing silent prayers while I braved the sweet musty smell of death. And man, was I wrong! There was no way I could ever get used to that. It was as if, during the night, the walls had given up every bit of odor they'd been hoarding over the last century and a half. Believe me, I worked fast.

I bounded straight up the stairs—well, a woman my height doesn't bound up anything, but you get my drift. When I reached the second floor I made a mad dash through the master bedroom to C.J.'s private bath. Of course it was silly of me, but I had a strong feeling that I was being watched. And why wouldn't I? One of the walls downstairs had eyes *and* ears, didn't it?

Fortunately, the stealthy renovators had limited their activities to the third floor. Just as one can tell the age of a tree by counting its rings, the peeling layers of paint and wallpaper in C.J.'s private bathroom marked the decades. As fascinating as that history was, I headed straight for her plumbing fixtures. First I tapped them, then I managed to unscrew a faucet handle and test its weight in my hand. Lacking my reading glasses, I located a magnifying make-up mirror and held the fixture up to it. The reflection was, of course, backwards—K41—but it told me everything I needed to know. The handle was solid gold.

"Lord have mercy!" I said aloud.

"Mercy!" Either there was an echo in the room, or the walls did indeed possess another mouth.

I didn't stay to find out. I high-tailed my hiney out of there faster than greased lightning.

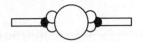

21

Thank heavens Mama was still in C.J.'s garden, sitting in one of the wrought iron chairs. Alas, she was not alone. Gladys Kravitz with the marshmallow chin was sitting in the other chair, and the two of them were laughing like nobody's business.

Despite the fact that I was panting like a fox at the end of a chase, they neither heard nor saw me coming. I waited until there was a lull in the laughter before speaking. Both women jumped, and when their bottoms reconnected with the metal chairs, I could feel the thunk on the brick pavers beneath my feet.

"Land o' Goshen!" Mama cried. "Abby, you about scared us to death."

Gladys Kravitz was breathing as hard as the aforementioned fox, but she didn't say a word, preferring to glare at me over that edible chin.

"Sorry, Mama." I turned to Gladys. "Sorry, ma'am."

The woman grunted.

"Abby," Mama rasped, "I want you to meet my

new friend, Gloria Krantz. Gloria, this hooligan is my daughter, Abigail Wiggins Timberlake Washburn."

Gloria Krantz? Well, that certainly wasn't far off the mark. But who was Mama kidding? I hadn't been gone more than five minutes, and she'd made friends with C.J.'s busybody neighbor. You can see why I have to look out for her. I'm talking about Mama, of course. C.J.'s neighbor was quite capable of looking out for herself, and everyone else in the neighborhood.

I nodded curtly. "We've met."

"Yes, we have," Miss Krantz said. "Your daughter came skulking around the house the other day."

"I wasn't skulking, ma'am."

"And then the police showed up. I couldn't see everything that was going on—"

"Try as you might."

"—but I'm pretty sure there was a scuffle of some kind, because one of the police officers came out with her hands over her face. There was blood everywhere."

"I didn't do it!" I wailed. And I didn't. One doesn't get a bloody nose just from being whacked on the behind. Can I help it if Officer Cheech bumped her nose trying to get it out of that musty hole?

Miss Krantz smirked. "I heard that the officer required thirty-seven stitches to close the gash, and had to have her nose set in some sort of a special cast."

"You heard no such thing," I snapped.

Mama gasped. "Abby, be civil!"

"But Mama, it isn't true."

"Abigail!" Mama gave me a look that could have turned milk into cottage cheese. Then she turned to her new friend and smiled sweetly. "Gloria here invited me to a party Saturday night. Isn't that nice?"

"What?"

"Abby, are you losing your hearing?"

"No, ma'am, but Gloria claims her family has lived in Charleston for three hundred years. I think maybe it's you who heard wrong."

"Oh no, your mother heard right." Gloria stood and tried to smooth the wrinkles on her linen skirt. "See you at six, Mozella?"

"With bells on," Mama said, and twittered shamelessly.

"No bells, please," Gloria said, and walked imperiously away without another word.

I dropped Mama off at the house, picked up a diet cola and a handful of Hershey's dark chocolate and almond Nuggets—it was going to be a long ride—and headed out to see Thelma Maypole again. I tried to call her, but got the sort of busy tone that indicated she was on the computer. No matter. Although it was hot enough outside to fry spit, it was also a beautiful, cloudless day.

The Ashley River sparkled like Greg's eyes, and small sailboats were out in force, practicing for an upcoming regatta. On a day like this, I feel the urge to get down on my knees and thank my Maker that I now live within the smell of salt water. But it is generally unsafe to drive while kneeling, so instead I sang the hymn "Joyful, Joyful, We Adore Thee"— well, those words of it which I could remember. It had been a while since I'd been to church.

I made good time on Bohicket, but hit a snag at the entrance to Kiawah Island. I had not been able to get through to Thelma when I called from home, and the guard at the gate insisted that my name had to be on the list of expected visitors. I asked the guard to call Thelma on my behalf, which she did. Alas, the line was still busy.

I would have tried calling Thelma on my cell phone, but I had left it at home on my kitchen counter when I picked up the chocolate. Feeling somewhat desperate, I implored the guard to let me through anyway. I even offered her a piece of chocolate. Not only did the woman refuse, but adamantly so. I will not disparage the guard's origins, other than to say that she was apparently from up the road a piece and may not have liked my accent.

Thus I was forced to backtrack several miles to the nearest public phone just outside the Piggly Wiggly. I like using public telephones about as much as I enjoy chewing gum scraped off the sidewalk, but I had no choice. There were two machines, one a little less grease-smeared than the other, and after fumbling around in a purse messier than a teenager's dresser drawers, I managed to locate enough change.

The static was horrible, but Thelma picked up on the first ring. "Hello?"

"Ms. Maypole, this is Abigail Washburn—Mozella's daughter."

"I don't have a daughter. You must have a wrong number."

"I know you don't have a daughter, ma'am. I'm Mozella Wiggins's daughter." I shouted so loud that a woman pushing a buggy full of groceries to her car veered away from me, glancing anxiously over her shoulder.

Thelma Maypole hung up on her end.

I switched to the greasier phone. I had just enough coins to make one call. This time, however, I got another busy signal.

"Damn!" I said a few other choice words as well, words a Southern lady of good breeding ought never to utter.

"Abby, is that you?"

I dropped the phone and whirled. Thelma Maypole was standing not two feet away. The sunlight glinting off those hexagonal glasses was blinding. I looked away to spare my eyesight.

"Miss Maypole, you can't be here. I just called your house, and you were on the phone."

She laughed politely. "I haven't been home all

morning, Abby. And please, call me Thelma. I thought we agreed."

"But I just called your house—like just seconds ago."

Wrinkles appeared above the weird lenses. "Constance!"

"I beg your pardon?"

"The maid. Constance comes in three mornings a week, supposedly to clean. She does a terrible job, though—just pushes the dust around. Frankly, I've been trying to work up the courage to fire her. This might be the straw that broke the camel's back—although an earlier version of that proverb has it feathers breaking a horse's back. Speaking of horses, did you know that the horse family evolved mainly in the Americas, then spread to Europe via the land bridges, but became extinct on this side of the Atlantic between eight and ten thousand years ago? It wasn't until the Spanish explorers brought horses here in the early fifteen hundreds that the circle was complete."

"No ma'am, I didn't know that. Ma'am—I mean Thelma, do you mind if we continue this conversation at your house?"

"My house?" She looked alarmed, but sounded pleased.

"I was just coming to see you. Like I said, I tried to call."

"Will you be staying for lunch?"

"Well—"

"And of course I have plenty of room, should you decide to spend the night."

I'm sure I looked alarmed. "I was thinking more along the lines of a brief conversation. We can talk right here, if you don't mind."

"Very well." There was no disguising the disappointment in her voice. "But I have a few things to pick up in the Pig. Will you at least walk with me?"

"It would be my pleasure."

I meant it. It is always a pleasure to shop at the Pig, as we fondly refer to the Piggly Wiggly supermarkets. Many of them play classical music, and there is usually free coffee by the door, and oftentimes doughnuts or samples of cake.

We were in luck. The bakery department had left out a plate of glazed doughnuts and there were thermoses of chicory-flavored coffee as well as regular. I poured cups of chicory for both of us and snatched a doughnut. While I was pouring, Thelma Maypole downed an entire doughnut and reached for a second.

"Thelma," I said, and moved away from the door in hopes that she would follow, which she did. "Thelma, I learned something very interesting yesterday."

"You too? Did you know that half of the world's six thousand, eight hundred languages face extinction by the end of this century?"

"I did not know that. But—"

"For instance, there are only six people left who speak Arikapu."

"Ari—what?"

"It's a language spoken in the Amazon jungle."

"Well, that is indeed very interesting, almost as interesting as the fact that you once owned Jane Cox's house."

We'd been strolling past the deli counter, which was fortunate, because I was able to beg some paper towels from the woman filling up the olive bins. My bit of news seemed to have caused Thelma to spill her chicory coffee down her ample bosom.

I let her do the dabbing. "So it's true?" I asked.

"Abby, she's not going to sue, is she?"

"Why would she do that?"

"I didn't know what else to do." Thelma handed me a wad of shredded towels. "It's not like I could prove there was a ghost. I don't think anybody can, can they? I asked Chiz—I even checked with my lawyer. Neither of them seemed to know the answer, so I did what I had to do. I sold the damn place." She took a deep breath. "So sue me. I couldn't live in that house any longer. Not with all the wailing going on. Besides, I had my eye on this Kiawah property."

"Relax," I said. "No one's going to sue—not to my knowledge. I just found it interesting that you neglected to mention owning Jane's house."

"It didn't seem important." She picked at some of the paper remnants on her chest. "Abby, a word of advice to the wise is sufficient—that's what my mother used to say. So take it from me, someone who knows.

Don't ever buy a house way out someplace where you don't know anyone. It isn't that easy to make friends, especially when you've reached a certain age."

"I'll keep that in mind. So, Thelma, how long did you live in that house on Colonial Lake?"

"Oh, I was born and raised there."

"Come again?"

"Abby, do you have a hearing problem? It is not at all uncommon for someone our age, you know. The earliest hearing aids consisted of—"

"Thelma, I don't think we're quite the same age, and no, I do not have a hearing problem. I just can't believe you waited so long to sell that house, if you couldn't stand living there."

"Well, I had no choice, you see. I had to wait until my parents died, and Daddy died only last year. He was born and raised in that house as well. It would have killed him to leave."

I left the irony of that alone. "So how long was this house in your family?"

"Since before the war." We had reached the bakery department, where we discovered a plastic tray of sugar cookies waiting to be devoured by children with dirty fingers, and adults who couldn't stick to their diets. Thelma and I each had one. Then she had a second.

"I suppose you're referring to the War Between the States," I said, with my back to the bakery. The sugar cookies were the best I'd ever tasted.

"Oh yes," she said, and reached around me for another cookie. "My great-great-great-granddaddy, Silas MacGregor, built the house, and passed it on to his son Bruce MacGregor."

"MacGregor? But you're a Maypole!"

"My grandmother, Fanny MacGregor, was an only child. She married a Maypole."

"Your great-great-granddaddy Bruce—is he the one whose daughter, Sarah, took up with a house slave? And then when Sarah became pregnant, her daddy killed her?"

Thelma hung her head. It may have been shame, or maybe just to get a better view of the walnut-topped brownies in the glass case.

"That's conjecture, Abby. Nobody can prove that."

I reached out and patted her arm. It felt as cool as the brownie case.

"Thelma, dear, I found a body of a woman stuffed in the kitchen wall of your old digs."

She pulled her arm away and turned to face me. "Is this a joke?"

"No, ma'am. I've asked the police to have tests run to see if she was pregnant."

She continued to face me for what seemed like several minutes. I can only assume she was staring straight ahead in shock.

"Well," she finally said, "one doesn't have any control over one's ancestors, does one?"

"Not unless the New Age take on reincarnation is

right. In which case, according to some of the authors I've read, we pick the circumstances of our birth, in order to work through certain issues."

"And you believe that?"

"I find it interesting to contemplate. I've already concluded I must have been a tall, but arrogant, blond in my last life."

Thelma smiled weakly. "About this body—what will happen to it?"

"I don't know. You might want to contact Sergeant Scrubb in homicide. If it turns out to be who I think it is, maybe they'll let you bury her in a family plot."

She nodded. "If I planned a memorial service, would you come?"

"Absolutely. I'll even wear that dress with the hoop skirt again, if you want."

"I don't think that will be necessary, but thanks for offering. And thanks for telling me this in the first place. In a strange way it's comforting."

"Closure? That kind of thing?"

She nodded again, but she'd turned, and this time I'd bet my life on the fact she was staring at a lemon cheese cake. Either that, or the Black Forest cake next to it.

I pulled her into the produce section. I still had more business to discuss.

"Those tiles I found behind the refrigerator the night Madame Woo-Woo was murdered—were they always there?"

She was turned sideways to me, staring forlornly at

the bakery department. I could see stubby lashes blinking behind the strange lenses.

"I suppose they were. Abby, I really didn't pay much attention to that old house."

"But Thelma, you're a very bright woman, who seems to know something about everything. And you've been to Portugal!"

"Yes, that's true," she said without a hint of modesty. "I do know something about most things, but like I said, I always hated that house. I guess I never looked closely at those tiles."

"Who painted them orange?"

"Mama." She gave up on the bakery and began grazing on several varieties of seedless grapes. "Did you know that oranges have to be picked when they're fully ripe, because unlike a lot of other fruits the process doesn't continue once they leave the tree? That's why orange growers get so stressed when there is an early frost."

"Why, I didn't know that." The sarcasm dripping from my voice was enough to turn the sweetest, ripest orange into instant marmalade. "Did *you* know that the bathroom fixtures in the master suite of your old home were solid gold?"

She stared at me—well, I'm pretty sure she did. "No. But it doesn't surprise me. Mama and Daddy both liked nice things."

I couldn't very well ask the woman if she'd been having second thoughts, and had been ripping off the new owner of her ancestral home. Besides, Thelma neither looked, nor acted, like a woman who needed money.

"Thelma, when y'all were remodeling the third-floor bathrooms, who changed out the fixtures?"

She picked up a gala apple, and I held my breath, hoping she'd dare to take a bite. I've always admired a gutsy woman.

"That's the job I wanted, Abby, but we drew names out of a jar, and I got to refinish the dining room floor. I had to rent an electric sander—"

"Thelma, *please*. Just tell me who was responsible for the powder room."

Thelma set the apple down. "Ella."

"By herself?"

"Yes, and it took her forever—almost two weeks. We kept kidding her that she was spending her time in there writing a novel."

"Hmm. Thelma, I hope you don't mind if I ask you a personal question about your family."

The hexagons pointed straight down at me, and then she jerked her head. A lady in the nearby poultry corner was cooking up teriyaki chicken in an electric Dutch oven. I could sympathize with Thelma, torn as she was, between fruit and fowl.

"Let's get a sample," I suggested, "and then I'll ask."

She polished off three to my one. "Okay, Abby, what is this personal family question? It doesn't have to do with my Uncle Varney's time in Africa, does it?"

"No—well, maybe it does. Tell me about that."

She sighed, even as she eyed the seafood counter. "He went to Africa as a missionary—but this was a long time ago, when I was just a baby. Uncle Varney was Mama's youngest brother, by the way. Anyway, something went wrong out there—sunstroke, or something—and Uncle Varney took up living with a herd of baboons. When the British found him—this was Kenya—he had moved his way up through the ranks and was the alpha male. Baboons do that, you see—have alpha males and alpha females, sort of like wolves. But of course they're not wolves, so the patterns aren't the same. Now, where was I?"

"You were telling me about the Brits finding your uncle with the monkeys."

"Ah yes. Well, Uncle Varney had forgotten all his English, and the Swahili he'd been forced to learn to qualify as a missionary. The only way he could communicate was to bark like a baboon. That's what they do, you know—bark."

"So he barked at the Brits," I said, anxious to move the story along. "Then what?"

"Well, they tried to extricate him from the herd, but they couldn't. So they shot him. It was for his own good, you understand. They only meant to wound him, but alas, it was fatal. They shipped Uncle Varney back to Charleston in a sealed coffin. Someone in customs insisted on opening it, and boy, were they in for a surprise."

She paused dramatically, so I obliged. "What kind of surprise?"

"Uncle Varnie had grown a tail!"

"Thelma, dear, how well do you know Jane Cox?" We'd reached the seafood department and she took two samples of crab spread on crackers, and handed me one. "I met her that once—the night of the séance."

"Well, I think you two would make good friends."

"Oh?"

"Yes, I think you have a lot in common."

It's always disconcerting—what's more, it's downright unfair—when you can't see someone's eyes. Still, I could tell that the prospect of making a new friend appealed to this bright and eccentric woman. Now, if only I could prove she wasn't Madame Woo-Woo's killer.

We entered the meat department where a perky matron was handing out pieces of Hebrew National hot dogs impaled on brightly colored toothpicks. Thelma took two, handed me one, and helped herself to another from the plate.

"Abby, I had a wonderful idea. When I'm done shopping, why don't you follow me back to the island for lunch?"

I declined the kind offer. If I continued to follow her around the store until her shopping was done, there wouldn't even be room in my stomach for a glass of water. Besides, I had a new lead to follow.

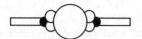

22

Curiously, Ella Nolte didn't seem surprised to see me. "It's you," she said, and beckoned me in.

"Miss Nolte, I wonder if I might have a few more minutes of your time."

"I knew you'd be back. In fact, I thought you'd be back a lot sooner."

"I'm afraid you've lost me."

She arranged her lips in what a charitable person might call a smile. "No doubt you've done a little snooping—you told me you would—and discovered that this author business is not all it's cracked up to be."

"Excuse me?"

"Don't play games with me, Mrs. Washburn. I'm flat broke, and you know it."

"Actually, I didn't—not until now."

"But you must have had an idea. I'm sure you stopped in at Waldenbooks in Charleston Place. Or Barnes & Noble and Books-A-Million up in North

Charleston. I bet you couldn't find a single copy of my books. Am I right?"

"I didn't look for your books. But I will," I quickly added.

"Don't bother, because you won't find any. My backlist has been dropped, and I haven't had a contract in three years."

"I'm sorry to hear that."

She had yet to ask me to sit, and that nose swept the length of my body like a metal detecting wand. "You're not here to rub it in?"

"I assure you, I'm not."

"Then have a seat." She threw herself on a chair. "It's a precarious business, that's all I can say. One day you're hot, and the next you're not. Tastes change, and then where are you? Sometimes I wish I'd listened to my mother."

"And what did she say?"

"Be an undertaker. Everyone dies."

I laughed agreeably.

"Laugh if you want, but Mama had steady work until the day she died."

"She was an undertaker?"

"She was an embalmer's assistant, and she did makeup on the deceased. But the big money, she said, was in owning your own home."

By that, I assumed she meant funeral home. But how fitting for the daughter of an embalmer's assistant to wind up as a mystery and horror writer. Well, they say, write what you know best, and no doubt young Ella had been weaned on talk of the dead.

As much as I would have liked to ask her about her childhood, I had work to do. I smiled pleasantly, and then pretended to start, as if I'd just remembered something.

"Oh, you'll never guess who I ran into at the Pig."

"Which Pig?"

Darn those mystery writers, always demanding details. "The Piggly Wiggly down near Kiawah Island."

"You just don't *run into* someone down there," Ella sniffed. "You're back to playing amateur sleuth, aren't you?"

"I'm only an amateur because I'm not being paid. I assure you that I'm quite capable of thinking like a professional."

"Ha, ha!" Actually, it was more of a bark. Perhaps it just slipped out, because she seemed as surprised by her outburst as I was. Nonetheless, she'd sounded like I imagined Thelma's Uncle Varney sounded when he was yapping it up with the baboons.

I wanted to tell her that being a hack writer didn't qualify her either, but shooting myself in the foot, while intensely interesting, has never been fun. Instead, I reached deep into my bag of social niceties and pulled out a lame smile of my own.

"Anyway," I said, barely moving my lips, "Thelma Maypole was telling me about how y'all divvied up the work at Jane Cox's house."

"She complained about having to redo the dining room floor, right?"

"Not exactly. What I—"

"It used to be her house, you know. The May-poles—all of them—let that beautiful old house just fall apart. Why shouldn't she get the toughest job? What I can't believe is that we let your mother talk us into fixing up the place. But she is charming, I'll grant you that."

"Mama, or Thelma?"

"Mozella."

"Yeah, she can charm a snake out of its basket. But back to Thelma—she said your job was the third-floor bathrooms."

"And that was no small task either. I scraped away five coats of paint on one wall, and three applications of wallpaper on the other walls. And the bottom two layers were the old-fashioned kind of paper that you couldn't just steam away."

"And you changed out the faucets," I said, trying not to sound accusatory.

"So what if I did? They were old and needed re-placing."

"Did you throw them out?"

"No, I planted them in my garden. I hope to grow faucet trees."

I can't stand sarcasm—at least not when it's di-rected at me. "Make sure you water them well."

"Of course I threw them out. They were old and scratched."

"They were also solid gold."

"What?" She recoiled, and the impressive nose retreated half a zip code.

"If they were anything like the ones upstairs, they were stamped 14 K."

She was on her feet. "Are you accusing me of stealing them? Is that what this is all about?"

"No, ma'am."

She may not have heard me. Next thing I knew she'd grabbed a book and threw it at me. Fortunately it was a very slim volume, barely more than a pamphlet, and didn't really hurt.

I picked it up. *Almanac of Intelligent Book Critics* the title read.

"This any good?" I asked calmly.

"Out! Get out of my house now!" she shrieked.

I was happy to oblige.

I stopped by the house to retrieve my cell phone. On the way there I got stuck behind a horsedrawn carriage and a garrulous tour guide, so I had some time to think. If the autopsy showed that Golda Feinstein was pregnant, then in my book Chisholm Banncock IX had the strongest motive. Just how he did it was another question. Perhaps he had some old family recipe for poison; no doubt something his ancestors used to get rid of their rivals in the Middle Ages. At any rate, he was smart, quite capable of doing a little research. And killing off his pregnant, lower-class girlfriend in a roomful of eccentric and somewhat contentious people was positively brilliant. *Assuming* he did it.

Dr. Francis Lloyd Whipperspoonbill had motive as well. The urge for revenge is one of the strongest of human emotions, and unfortunately, there are a whole lot of folks out there who don't wait for it to be served up cold. Madame Woo-Woo had essentially outed the man before he was ready. How hard would it be for a veterinarian to come up with a lethal substance to dab on a cassette recorder button? About as hard, in my book, as it was to clean a kitty litter tray.

Thelma Maypole had a reason to wreak revenge; but on the doctor, not Madame Woo-Woo. Still, the woman was nuttier than a pecan pie, and I had my doubts she wouldn't stop at implicating her ex-fiancé in a murder. A woman scorned—well, that's one cliché that's true. And this woman knew at least a little something about everything. Coming up with a poison would be a piece of cake for her—perhaps a doughnut, and several cookies as well.

Ella Nolte definitely had a mean streak, as did Hugh Riffle. But Hugh looked to be rolling in dough, while Ella appeared to have outlived her means. I'd always thought writers were rich, but apparently only some are. If Ella discovered that the old Maypole mansion held undisclosed treasures, she might have plotted a way to get her key-tapping fingers on them. She was, after all, an experienced plotter. But why would she kill Madame Woo-Woo? As a diversion? If so, that was yet another failed story line. No wonder her books weren't available at Barnes & Noble.

And what about Madame Woo-Woo? What did I know about her, except that she was an accomplished hustler, with a small H, who had been orphaned at a relatively young age, and had a brother—wait! Back to that orphan angle. Her parents were both antique dealers. She was raised in a home of historic and beautiful things. Even the trailer she shared with her brother was fabulously furnished. Perhaps her expert eye had zeroed in on some valuable object, like the tiles, and she had shared her observation with one of the Heavenly Hustlers.

Let's say the Hustler in question was desperately strapped for cash and thought she could sneak past the rest of the herd—but only if Madame Woo-Woo kept her big trap shut. The poorest Hustler that came to mind was the haughty author, who was obviously living way beyond her means. The next poorest, and this was only conjecture, had to be the veterinarian. Everyone knows they don't make as much money as people doctors. Of course, he was old money, but that's been known to run dry. Thelma Maypole was only an investment counselor, but she was old money too—so old, she couldn't see it in front of her hexag-onal glasses. Chisel-cheeked Chiz was loaded, there was no getting around that, which brought me right back to the Riffles. They *could* be living beyond their means, but I doubted it. Not with all the turnover that bizarre business of his did, at least according to the TV commercials.

Suppose that Lothario decided to dump her? What *would* an aging beauty queen do under those circum-stances? Try to find work posing for wrinkle-removal ads? Do television commercials for gentle laxatives? Or maybe take the laxative commercial one step fur-ther and advertise adult diapers? At any rate, divorced women are often at the bottom of the financial heap—wait just one cotton-picking minute!

The evening I first met Sondra Riffle she was wear-ing a brightly colored frog pin on her lapel. And when I visited her in the elegant but palatial house on the Battery, there was a terrarium in the powder room, along with Hugh's car stuff. Undoubtedly the car mo-tif was his idea, but the terrarium could have been hers. And there were live icky things in it too. I didn't look closely at the time, but those could have been frogs. Somehow I'd gotten the impression they were salamanders.

The horsedrawn carriage I'd been stuck behind got out of my way. I'm ashamed to say this, but I broke the speed limit getting the rest of the way home.

Mama wasn't home, but there was at least one message on my machine. I decided to ignore it until after I'd made my call.

"Scrubb," he said, picking up on the first ring.

His quick response caught me off guard. "Uh— Abby Timberlake—no, I mean Abby Washburn. You know who I mean. Did Greg call you?"

"Yes, ma'am."

"*And?*"

"And I called you and left a message. Didn't you get it?"

"I didn't check. Just tell me, please, was Golda Feinstein pregnant."

"Abby, you know I can't answer that directly. Let's just say that, as things stood at the time of her death, she would *not* have been shopping for baby clothes."

"Aha! And was the corpse I found in the wall missing a finger?"

He hesitated. "It's not like the corpse has any living kin—well, not of her generation at any rate."

"And?"

"That's the damnedest thing, Abby. How did you know?"

"Family legends usually contain at least a kernel of truth. Was *she* pregnant?"

"As a matter of fact, there was a small fetus. The coroner estimates it was three to four months old at the time of its death."

"The mother's name was Sarah MacGregor."

"Is that a fact?" He cleared his throat. "Sorry, I'm sure it is. You never cease to amaze me."

"I hope my husband feels the same way."

"You bet he does."

I was pleased to hear envy in his voice, and filled him in on what I knew of the MacGregor-Maypole family history. He thanked me and promised to let me know as soon as possible if the remains could be released to Thelma Maypole for burial. When our conversation ended, I scooped by my errant cell phone, gave a reluctant Dmitri a kiss on each whiskery cheek, and dashed out the door. Only one piece in the puzzle remained to be fitted.

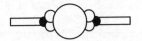

23

You can usually find a spot to park along the seawall on Murray Boulevard, the next street down from South Battery. Tourists seem to ignore these spots and use the city garages a blister or two away. Perhaps they assume that parking will be tight, if it exists at all, down where the Ashley and Cooper form the Atlantic. But it's there, trust me. Oops, have I spilled the beans?

My plan was to park next to the seawall, give my regards to the newly birthed ocean, then walk the short block through White Point Gardens to Sondra Riffle's house. However, as I stood on the sidewalk, waiting for yet another horsedrawn carriage to pass before I crossed the street, I heard someone call my name.

I knew it wasn't an owl, given that it was broad daylight. But I would never, in a million years, have expected it to be a buzzard. A buzzard named Buford. He was sitting on a park bench, his arm around a woman I'd never seen. I am not generally mean-spirited, and I don't mean to bad-mouth anyone, especially a stranger, but this was the homeliest woman I'd ever laid eyes on. Since I promise to go to Mama's church and confess personally to the priest, please allow me the following observation. The woman Buford was clutching had the body of a manatee, the face of a bulldog, and I'd seen better hair on roadkill. She was *not* Buford's style.

Buford's mama was dead, I knew that. Perhaps the woman was an aunt, or a favorite cousin. She might even have been a very wealthy client he was attempting to comfort.

"Abby," he called again, and rose to his feet. "Come here. I want you to meet someone."

I trotted over, but only out of curiosity. The closer I got, the homelier the woman became. This promised to be a very interesting encounter.

"Abby, I want you to meet my wife, Loretta. Honey," Buford said to the woman, "this is my first wife, Abigail."

You could have knocked me over with a feather. "Get out of town!" I cried. I didn't intend for those words to escape my lips, and I clapped my hands over my mouth in mortification.

Loretta struggled to her feet. She towered over me, of course, but she loomed over Buford as well. She must have been at least six feet, and I'd be willing to bet small change she was a couple of inches taller than that. At least, when viewed from this angle, the bulldog face was smaller, and the roadkill hair all but disappeared in the clouds.

She held out a hand the size of New Jersey. "Pleased to meet you," she said in that state's charming accent.

I did the proper thing and shook it. It was so damp that, given our location, it may well have been a third source of the Atlantic.

"Married?" I asked. I know, that was rude as well, but Buford had said that he was going to do the right thing and tie the knot sometime, not that he had already strangled her.

"This morning," she said, and gave me a big grin, which confirmed that she had at least a few teeth.

"Congratulations to you both."

"Abigail—may I call you that?"

"Abby's better."

"Abby, do you think we could talk?"

"Sure. I'm in a bit of a hurry now—but maybe tonight the two of you could come over for drinks." I wanted to slap myself into the next county for saying that, but part of me meant it. I wanted Mama and Greg to see, for themselves, Buford's new wife. Mere words were not going to suffice.

"Please," she said, gazing down at me with those bulging eyes, "could we talk now. We're going back home this afternoon, you see. It will only take a minute."

"Honey," Buford said, and laid a manicured hand on one of her bare white arms, "maybe y'all could chat the next time we're in town. Abby here is a very busy woman."

"Not that busy," I said, partly just to be contrary, and partly out of morbid fascination. What could the giantess possibly have to say that couldn't wait a decade or two? I know that if our positions were reversed, I'd avoid her like last week's fish.

"Wonderful!" Loretta said. She reached down and grabbed one of my hands. Then she pulled me along as if I were her child, and we'd inadvertently entered a candy store.

There is a wrought iron gazebo in the park, and she steered me toward that. I knew Buford had to be beside himself with frustration, because we were out of earshot. When we reached the gazebo I turned and saw him sitting there, as helpless and forlorn as a little boy sitting outside the school principal's office, when his mother has already gone in.

Loretta squeezed my hand. Fortunately, I don't have to type for a living.

"Buford says such wonderful things about you."

"He does?"

"Oh yes. How you were the perfect mother—" she paused. "He doesn't say that exactly, but I know that's what he means."

"Loretta—"

"I know what you're going to say, Abby."

"You do?"

"You're going to say 'watch him like a hawk.' "

"Or like a snake."

Her laugh was like marbles rattling in a jar. "Timber snake. He told me you call him that sometimes."

"Well, only when he's really pissed me off—which is about every time I've seen him over the last three years."

"Abby, I know he's a slimebucket, but then again, so am I."

That took me by surprise. "No, you're not!"

"But I am. I cheated with Buford on his wife Tweetie, didn't I? Abby, I'm not here to make excuses. I just wanted to reassure you that, since I will be having some contact with your children, I will not be bad-mouthing you."

"Thanks." It felt strange to be expressing gratitude to someone for not doing what they shouldn't be doing in the first place. That I was even having this conversation just goes to show how complicated the institution of marriage is. When that knot is untied, the result is more than two loose strings finally dangling independent of each other. There are frayed edges and loose filaments galore to contend with.

She gave my hand another bone-breaking squeeze. "Well, I just wanted you to know that. I don't want us to be enemies."

Enemies? It wouldn't have occurred to me to think of her as a potential enemy. She hadn't—couldn't—

take anything away from me, and there was nothing of hers that I wanted. In fact, despite her hulking size, she seemed sadly vulnerable.

"Watch your back, dear," I said in all kindness. "More importantly, watch Buford's back. The beast with two backs is his hobby, and he likes to indulge in it with strangers."

"I understand," she said, and began pulling me back to Buford.

I left the happy couple sitting on the park bench and, narrowly escaping the hooves of a horse, scooted across the street to interview Sondra one last time. I had to ring twice, and when she answered the door she was wearing the same pink silk PJs she'd been wearing the last time I saw her. Perhaps all her real clothes were out at the cleaners.

"Please forgive me for just dropping by like this," I said. A real Charlestonian would probably have sent a note first—possibly by horsedrawn carriage. "I was in the neighborhood and thought of something I wanted to ask you."

She stared at me. She wasn't wearing any makeup this time, and it was painfully obvious that her days as Miss Kudzu, and Miss Regional Okra, were long gone. When she pursed her lips, the wrinkles made me think of a Spanish fan.

"Is this about Madame Woo-Woo's murder again?"

"I'm afraid so."

"Abby, this is getting to be very tedious." I could smell gin on her breath.

"Oh, but it's not what you think. The police have found her killer." Well, they would soon, if I had anything to do about it, so it was only a pseudo-lie.

She blinked, and then smiled almost as an afterthought. "Please, come in."

I followed her through the grand hall lined with black marble statues and into the salon. I chose the same Louis XV fauteuil chair to sit in that I had before. As before, I coveted the cream fabric with its pale pink roses on vinelike stems.

She sat opposite me. "Please, tell me everything."

"Well—uh, excuse me, but before I get started on the juicy details, may I use your powder room again?"

"Please, be my guest. You remember where it is?"

I assured her that I did, and trotted off in that direction. Even though I knew what to expect, the over-the-top car theme was just as startling as the first time I'd seen it. Even more so. Instead of a terrarium on the vanity, there was a model of a hearse. It had a cord coming from one side that plugged into a socket, and the wheels on the hearse were constantly spinning. Every now and then the back doors of the model hearse would open, and a small plastic coffin would slide partway out. Then the coffin popped back in like a cuckoo bird, and the doors slammed shut. It was so fascinating that I momentarily forgot this was a replacement for the terrarium.

The terrarium! I glanced frantically around the room. Could I have just imagined it? Were the brightly colored icky things in it only a figment of my imagination? Not bloody likely. I'd stayed away from psychedelics in the seventies, unlike Mama, but that's a different story.

I lingered just long enough to give my visit legitimacy, then I flushed the toilet and ran the tap water for a few seconds. When I returned to the salon, Sondra was sitting where I'd left her, but this time she was holding a drink.

"Could I offer you something?" she asked.

"No, thanks. That's a really neat hearse thingamajig in there."

"Thanks, that belongs to Hugh."

"What happened to the terrarium?"

"Terrarium?"

"Yeah, that glass tank you had in there last time. The one with all the icky things in it."

She laughed softly. "Oh that! That was really an aquarium."

"Really? I could have sworn it had plants and land things in it. Anyway, what happened to it?"

"Like I said, it was an aquarium." Her words had sharp edges to them now. "It sprang a leak and the fish died. I threw it away."

There are times when the lack of evidence is every bit as damning as the evidence. This was one of those times. I wanted to stand up, point at her, and shout

"J'accuse!" Instead I arranged my lips in what was, at best, a tepid smile.

"I'm so disappointed to learn that it was only an aquarium. I've got this thing about frogs, you see. And I noticed you wearing a frog pin the other day, and I was hoping you were into them as well."

"Frogs? You mean like Kermit?"

"Well, him too. But I actually like real frogs. I always wanted to have a terrarium with those brightly colored frogs that come from South America."

She took a long sip of her drink, but said nothing. By the reaction on her face I could have been talking about the price Lutheran churches in Sweden have to pay for their hymnals.

"The only trouble is," I said, forced to take the plunge, "is that the brighter and more colorful the frog, the more likely it is to be poisonous."

I could have been talking about the price of hymnals in Norway for all she seemed to care. She looked blankly at me as she took another sip.

"Some South American Indian tribes used the poison to coat darts for their blowguns."

The aging beauty queen's face underwent an instant and remarkable transformation. Miss Regional Okra never looked like that. Maybe the first-runner up in the Miss Hell Swamp festival did, but definitely not Miss R.O.

"Now you've done it," she said through lips twisted in anger. "You've gone too far."

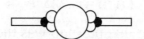

24

"What? I was just making pleasant conversation."

"No, you weren't." She drained her glass. "So, you've figured it out. I must say, Abby, you're smarter than I thought you were."

"Thank you."

"Now the question is, what do I do next?"

That was the same question I was asking myself. Sondra Riffle had much longer legs than I did, so a mad dash to the door was probably not going to save me. Perhaps, since my tongue had gotten me into this sticky wicket, it could get me out.

"A lot of people think beauty queens are dumb, but I always knew you were smart. One can tell just by talking to you."

"I have an IQ of 174. Unfortunately, Hugh doesn't give a damn about brains."

"Hugh is a jerk."

"You've got that right. But then, so am I. An idiot,

actually. Signing that pre-nup was the stupidest thing I ever did."

"But how were you to know your husband would cheat on you?" I was the idiot! The next time I went sleuthing—assuming there was a next time—I'd do well to first staple my tongue to the roof of my mouth.

Much to my relief, Sondra didn't seem the least bit surprised by my question. "Did he hit on you, too?"

"Well—"

"Although I must say I'm surprised; you're not exactly his type."

"What does that mean?"

"Let's just say he likes them a bit taller—more the beauty contestant type."

My unstapled tongue couldn't move fast enough. "Golda Feinstein was no beauty queen!"

"Isn't that the truth! Now that one really surprised me. I never would have guessed that bitch would have lasted so long. Maybe she really did have some sort of special powers."

"Ah, so it was a double motive. You got rid of your main rival, and the one person who knew what hidden treasures Jane Cox's house held."

Sondra stared at me again. "Speaking of surprises, you're just a bundle of them, aren't you, Abby?"

"I always loved *The Price Is Right*. Behind door number one—"

"I couldn't believe the good eye that bitch had. She waltzed right in the day before—your mama had me open the house for her, said she needed to get in for some damn reason—anyway, where was I?"

"The bitch's good eye."

"That's right. That good eye. The second she stepped into that house, she started enumerating its treasures. Some of the more obvious ones I could understand—like that Tiffany window on the stair landing. I was going to replace that with a nice double-paned sash in faux stained glass—now where was I?"

The drink, probably one of many, appeared to have affected her train of thought. Perhaps I stood a chance of escaping after all. I slid smoothly and quietly to my feet.

"You were still prattling on about the bitch's good eye. What else did she see?"

"The tiles! I still can't believe how quickly she zeroed in on them. Of course they extend all the way up the wall, but with all that hideous orange paint, and only the little patch behind the refrigerator exposed, I almost missed them myself." She held up her glass and tilted her head back so that the remnants of her drink could trickle down her throat.

That's when I made a run for it.

The next thing I knew my noggin felt like I'd been head-butting with a bighorn sheep. I had no idea where I was, but it was as dark as a stack of black cats. I strained to see something—maybe a star—but couldn't. I knew it was night only because I could hear tree frogs chirping.

"It's such a pleasant, relaxing sound, isn't it?" a disembodied voice said.

I forget what I tried to say, but it came out as a groan.

"Oh, I'm sure your head will hurt for a while," the voice said, and laughed.

"Sondra?"

"Like I said, you're pretty damn smart."

"What happened? Where am I?"

"You're in my third-floor attic, Abby. I'm afraid I beaned you with my gin glass. By the way, you owe me a new one."

It was then I realized I was lying on my side. I tried to sit, but couldn't. The crazy woman had put my hands behind my back and taped them to my feet. I was trussed like a calf about to be branded, only blindfolded as well.

I gasped in pain. "What do you plan to do?"

"Who, me? I don't plan to do anything. Those frogs you hear chirping will do it for me. You were right, Abby, some South American Indians do use toxins from frogs to poison their darts. One particularly toxic species is *Dendrobates auratus*, those cute little strawberry red guys you saw in the terrarium. Oh, and I've also got *Phyllobates terribilis*. Don't you just love that name? I know they're less than two inches long, but Abby, all that toxin has to do is get in your bloodstream and paralysis will set in. In a few minutes your heart will stop. Then it's bye-bye, Abby." She laughed insidiously.

"Are you saying that—"

"Yes, Abby, I think we're on the same page. I won't be doing you in. It's the cute little frogs that will be at fault. Incidentally, it's the males you hear chirping. It's their mating season and they're defending their new territories."

"Don't be ridiculous." Each word hurt like a blow to the head.

"I'm not the one being ridiculous, Abby. I've collected poison dart frogs ever since high school. How much do you know about them?"

"I meant you blaming it on the frogs. If anything does happen to me, it will be your fault, not theirs."

"I don't think I like your tone, Abby. You seem to forget that you are totally in my power now. I might not be able to control Hugh, but I sure the hell can control you." She laughed shrilly. "I'm a poet and don't know it!"

There was no point mincing words now. "You're crazy."

"Now, now, Abby, don't be unkind. You've heard of survival of the fittest, haven't you? Well, I just happen to be more fit than you. This is all about survival."

"You won't get away with it! Someday—even if it's two hundred years from now—someone will find me, and figure it was you."

"Don't you listen, Abby? I said my frogs were going to do you in, not me. I'm just laying the groundwork."

"Groundwork?"

"You know that glass you broke?"

"I didn't break it, you did. You threw it at me."

"Your head broke it, Abby, it's the same thing. Anyway, the toxins need to get in your bloodstream, or your saliva. Unfortunately I have no guarantee one will hop into your mouth—although it is possible. Therefore, I've taken the liberty of giving them a little assist. I've spread the pieces of broken glass around your body." She laughed softly. "Actually, I was feeling generous and broke a couple of extra glasses. Don't move too much, Abby, or you're likely to get cut. Move a little more and you might roll over one of my babies. Touch them with one of your cuts, and that will surely do the trick." She laughed again. "And thank you for wearing shorts, Abby. It's going to make the frogs' job so much easier. Oh, and I took the liberty of taking your phone and removing your sandals. I hope you don't mind. And such small sandals they were too. Wherever do you find them?"

"I'm not going to move, you bitch!"

"I was hoping you'd say that. I would hate for my froggies to die. I'll be putting some live ants in here with y'all—they eat live ants, you know—so they won't starve. I'm afraid you won't be quite as lucky."

So those were my choices. I could lie still and starve to death—never even trying to escape—or I could move. If I moved I'd risk lacerating my bare arms and legs, maybe even my cheeks. In the process I'd no doubt roll over one of the icky amphibians. Then I'd die of heart failure just like Madame Woo-Woo. Well, if I was going to die, I wanted to die with all the details.

"How did Golda Feinstein get the poison inside her system? Did you glue a shard of glass to the play button of the recorder?"

"No need. I just swabbed a nice thick layer of *Phyllobates terribilis* secretions on it. Then at some point she touched her mouth. People are forever touching mouths, eyes, and noses, Abby. That's the primary way colds are spread—from hands to face."

"But I touched that same button that evening."

"The best secretions are fresh, Abby. I waited until I arrived the night of the séance before applying the poisonous ooze. When everyone else was preoccupied with food—those were the worst ham biscuits I've ever tasted, by the way—I sneaked into the dining room and made my little deposit."

"Worst you've ever tasted?" I shouted. I foolishly struggled against my bonds for a few seconds. "You take that back, bitch!"

"Not as long as geese go barefoot. And while I'm at it, that was pretty bad cake too. Really, Abby, you and your mother should both enroll in a cooking class somewhere."

It was one thing to kick a pony when it's down, but

to keep kicking it when it was bound with rope and duct tape—well, there was no excuse for that. I racked my aching brain for a sufficiently worthy insult of my own. Alas, I took too long.

"Bye-bye, Abby," she said. "Good night, sleep tight, and don't let the bedbugs bite. But do let the frogs hop all over you." Then she slammed the door.

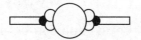

25

I lay still as a mummy in a collapsed pyramid. The only thing that moved was my heart, which threatened to burst from my chest. Hopefully, if that were the case, my heart would land on one of the poison dart frogs and squash it.

Around me, in all directions, came the peeps, chirps, and trills of horny, defensive frogs. You can bet I kept my eyes and mouth tightly closed. Maybe if I could just fall asleep, I'd wake up and find it had all been a dream, a nasty nightmare brought on by eating too much chocolate Häagen Dazs. I would, of course, have been eating the ice cream while watching a video with my husband Greg, who would have been massaging my feet at the time.

Maybe it was the blow to my head, or maybe it was the strain of the terror I was feeling, but I was actually very sleepy. I was on the verge of slipping under when I felt a soft plop on my exposed calf. It had the weight and texture of a handful of Gummy Bears. Instinctively I jerked, and the blob on my leg leaped away into the darkness. You can bet I screamed. In fact, I screamed so long and hard my throat and chest hurt. When I finally quit, except for a muffled echo, there were no sounds. Perhaps frogs had sensitive eardrums, and my shrieks had killed them all, or at least disabled them. But then again, did frogs even have ears?

I lay there in the dark for what seemed like hours, waiting for the frogs to resume their chirping, my muscles tensed against the feel of soft frog flesh on mine. But except for the pounding of my heart, and a rhythmic whoosh in my ears, the room was silent. Eventually I fell asleep, jerked myself awake a minute or two later, and fell asleep again. Finally, I succumbed to a deep sleep of utter exhaustion. As I was going under I dreamed that an angel appeared and swept me out of the room. She—it was definitely a female angel—told me I was on my way home, and that I'd wake up in my own bed. Before I got there, however, I had to pass through a very warm place.

I have no idea how long I was out, but when I awoke my circumstances had changed considerably; my hands and feet were untied, but most importantly, I was no longer blindfolded. I was not, however, back home in my bed.

"Well, well, Sleeping Beauty finally decided to wake up."

I blinked. Looking down at me was the Statue of Liberty. I blinked again.

"It still fits, doesn't it?"

"What?"

"The dress, you idiot. I wore this gown when I won Miss Congeniality in the Miss Cape Fear Shrimp and Grits Festival. It's my favorite, you know—prawn pink is my color, don't you think? Anyway, I would have worn it in the Miss Regional Okra pageant, except that some cracker judge spilled shrimp sauce on it."

My eyes were serving me better now. I could see that it was Sondra, not Miss Liberty, looming above me. She was wearing a stained pink gown that, contrary to her claim, didn't fit well at all. Bulges strained at the waist, and the madwoman's bosom and the dress's darts did not match up. Diagonally, from broad shoulder to bulging waist, she wore a sash. Crowning her head was a huge tiara, which must have looked quite stunning back in the days when its cheap faux crystals still glittered.

The sash had yellowed with age, making the gold letters on it hard to read. I tried sounding them out aloud.

"Miss Congenital—"

"That's congeniality," she snapped. "So, what do you think of your new digs?"

I hadn't seen my "old" digs, but I sat and took stock of my supposedly new surroundings. I was in for several big surprises. The first surprise was that I'd been lying on a cot with a mattress—albeit the mattress was so filthy I wouldn't have used it in an outdoor doghouse. The second surprise was even bigger; I was wearing a leg iron, which was chained to the cot.

"What the hell!"

Sondra smiled. "I can't have my guest just up and leave me now, can I?"

"I'm not your guest!"

"Why of course you are. You're in my house, aren't you?"

"Am I?" It appeared that I was in an attic room *somewhere*. The ceiling sloped sharply in one direction, and there were no windows, except for a series of very small, but deep, dormers. They were barely more than tubes that extended through the sloped ceiling and roof to the outside. In centuries past these miniature dormers might have served as air vents for slaves or indentured servants. Time had taken its toll on this seldom-used part of the house, and at least two of the tiny windows were missing their glass panes.

"This is a big house," Sondra said, stating the obvious. "There are twenty-four regular rooms, and then the attic. The attic has eight rooms. Hugh never comes up here—hates the stairs. In fact, he almost never even goes upstairs at all. I get to do anything I want with the attic. Of course in the summer it's too hot to do much of anything, even with the air-conditioning we installed a few years back."

That's when I first noticed how hot it was. Imagine,

if you will, climbing into a black car that has been parked in full sun all day. Sweat trickled down my sides, and my legs and arms were glistening. At least my legs weren't bleeding. It appeared I had missed the broken glass.

"There's air-conditioning up here?" I asked.

She nodded and pointed to a vent on the floor, about the size of a cereal box top. "Can't you feel it?"

"Cold air sinks."

"Well, it's there, and I wouldn't be ungrateful, if I were you. I'll be more than happy to close the vent."

"No, please don't! I just didn't notice it at first—but now I do."

"That's better, Abby. That's a more cooperative spirit. I mean, I could have put you in one of the rooms that didn't have any vents. Besides, I've got to save the coolest room for my frogs."

I glanced around. "Your frogs! I almost forgot about them. They're not in this room?"

"Oh no, I moved you during the night. I decided you posed too much of a threat to my babies."

"Your babies?"

"My poison dart frogs, you idiot! Abby, you're even slower than I thought."

"Well, it's hot—uh, not as cool as I'm used to." I screwed up the courage to ask the question I'd been too afraid to ask. "What do you plan to do with me?"

"Ha! Now that's a sensible question." She sighed. "It would have been easier if you'd just cooperated."

"You mean, quietly cut myself and waited for a frog to hop on board?"

"You don't need to be sarcastic, Abby. It doesn't become you. You've been a real strain, you know—I was hardly able to sleep all night. But," she said, her voice brightening. "I thought of a solution."

"You're going to let me go?" It never hurts to have a positive attitude.

"I'm going to hold you for ransom."

"What?"

"Abby, you've obviously got money—what with living South of Broad, and owning your own shop. I got some good stuff out of Jane Cox's house, but I think I can get even more for you."

I can't deny that I was flattered. Imagine, little ol' me being worth more than four-hundred-year-old Portuguese tiles, solid gold faucets, and who knows what else that home decorator had discovered with her eagle eye. There was one thing, however, that still concerned me.

"As soon as the ransom is paid," I said in my most nonchalant voice, "you're going to let me go, right?"

She laughed long and heartily. "Oh, Abby, you are so amusing at times. Of course I can't let you go."

"You plan to kill me?"

"Well, I'd have to now, wouldn't I?"

"*How?*"

"I'm a reasonable woman, Abby. I'm sure we can work out the details together."

"Death by chocolate?"

She didn't find that amusing. She stamped a long narrow foot, and the silly tiara tilted rakishly.

"You're wasting my time." She pointed to a blue plastic bucket in the corner. "There's your bathroom—I don't want you messing anything in here. You're going to have to scoot your bed over to use it."

"What about water? And food?"

"I'll take care of that later."

"Oh goody, room service."

"There's that sarcasm again, Abby. You know how much I hate it." She put her hands on her spreading hips, assuming a very un-beauty-queen-like pose. "On second thought, you won't be getting any food. Just water—if you're lucky. You'll need to be able to talk in case I have to put you on the phone."

"I'm sorry!"

"Too late, Abby." She took a last look around. "Enjoy your stay at Chez Riffle," she said, without a hint of humor. Then she spun on her six-inch heels, strode to the door, and slammed it behind her.

I heard the lock turn, and then the clicking of her stilettos, which grew fainter by the second. Once again I was enveloped by a silence almost as stifling as the heat.

The promised water was slow in coming. To conserve bodily fluids I lay quietly on the bed while I considered my options. I could drag the bed over to one of the miniature dormers—one with the glass missing—and shout for help. But what if Sondra heard me? Then it would be curtains for sure.

Another option was to drag the bed over to the door and jam the headboard under the doorknob. Then, if I could somehow free my foot from its shackle, I could call for help. Sondra might not be able to force the door open with the bed in the way. Silly me, why not free myself first, and then drag the bed to the door? But how was I going to free my foot? I couldn't exactly gnaw it off like an animal caught in a trap.

An animal caught in a trap! That's what I was. The only difference between this two-legged animal and a four-legged one in the woods, was that my leg was merely encased by metal, it wasn't punctured in multiple places by steel jaws. In that regard, I was a whole lot better off than the four-legged kind.

On the other hand, they say that we humans are the only creatures aware of our mortality. Assuming this is true—and it's a rather arrogant assumption, if you ask me—I was in one way worse off than my more furry brethren. I knew, beyond a shadow of a doubt, that I was at the mercy of a whacko who meant to follow through on her threat.

The third option was to somehow overpower her on her next visit. But since I didn't even have a shoe with which to konk her on the noggin, I didn't hold out much hope for that. I could try to hit her in the face with the plastic bucket, or its contents, but then what? As long as I remained shackled to the bed, I was at her mercy.

As I lay pondering my limited options, I began to hallucinate. Perhaps it was because I'd been thinking of small furry animals, but I distinctly heard my cat Dmitri meowing from somewhere above and behind me. At first it was a comforting sound, kind of like the surf, when the waves are up only a foot or so.

"Mama loves you too," I murmured. As long as there was no one there to document my behavior, there was no reason not to talk back to my hallucination. It's not like I was totally around the bend, like the first runner-up in the Miss Hell Swamp contest.

Dmitri, bless his fur-covered heart, talked back. In fact, he talked so loudly, and so continuously, I began to get annoyed. I tried to steer hallucination to a more soothing audio track, like the aforementioned small waves, but to no avail. Hallucinations, unlike daydreams, don't have a whole lot of maneuverability.

"Stop it, Dmitri!" I shouted.

The meowing stopped on command, only to be followed by a light thump on the floor, and the tinkle of a bell. Holy moly, now I was hallucinating about giant poison dart frogs. If one that big landed on me, I wouldn't even need abrasions to suffer its ill effects. But I'd heard a bell. Poison dart frogs from the Amazon probably don't wear bells around their necks, but cats sometimes do. And we were in the habit of attaching a bell to Dmitri's collar every time we let him outside, in order to give the birds he encountered a chance to escape.

Meowowow.

It was a distinctively Dmitri sound. I turned, daring to hope. Surely even the most exotic South American frogs were incapable of imitating cats, and my ten-pound bundle of joy in particular.

"Dmitri!" I cried. "It is you! You really are here!"

My big yellow tomcat raced across the room and leaped into my arms. I burst into tears. Oblivious to salt water splashing on him, Dmitri began to knead my thighs like they were twin loaves of dough. I babbled and blubbered while he purred. If this was a hallucination, then I had surely missed out on a lot of good stuff in the seventies by being a goody two-shoes.

Suddenly Dmitri froze. I didn't hear anything, but his ears were pinned back, every muscle in his body tensed. Then I heard the faint click of stiletto heels.

There are occasions in which time loses all meaning. It seemed like I was thinking in slow motion, and I don't remember actually deciding to do what I did— I just did it. I removed the bell on Dmitri's collar, crammed it into the pocket of my shorts, and replaced it with my wedding band. Then mustering strength I never knew I had, I dragged the bed beneath the nearest open dormer. Standing on the filthy mattress I lifted my bundle of joy to the small opening.

Dmitri was reluctant to leave. His back claws raked my hands while he struggled to get down.

"Please," I begged him, "go back home. Go see daddy—or grandma. Please!"

I heard the key turn in the lock and shoved him through the opening. "Go!"

The door swung open while I was still standing, my arms raised above my head. At least I'd been caught empty-handed.

"Abby, what the hell are you doing?" Sondra had changed into a blue gown. Her sash read: Miss Pine Bark Mulch.

"I'm exercising," I said, trying hard not to sound sarcastic.

"Why are you next to the window?"

"To get some air. I told you it was hot in here."

She grunted. "Here," she said, and set a clear plastic jug on the floor. "Your water."

"Thanks."

She turned, took several steps, and turned again. "It won't do you any good to shout for help. I have one of the deepest backyards South of Broad. Besides which, everybody's got their air-conditioners running. No one will hear you—except for me. If I hear you—well, then our time together is up."

"Yes, ma'am."

"Are you being sarcastic again, Abby?"

"No, ma'am."

I waited once more until the sound of her heels faded away. Then I shoved the bed in front of the door, and lay down to await my fate.

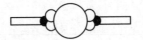

26

"It was less than eight hours," Greg said. He had his arm around me and gave me a squeeze that would have crumbled the bones of a woman who consumed fewer dairy products.

We were seated on a French Provincial loveseat in the Rob-Bobs' house, having just eaten a surprisingly edible meal prepared by Bob. Everything on the menu was recognizable except for the Twice-Baked Eel, which was discreetly hidden in cute little pastry puffs. I'd never had that dish before but, to my untrained palate, it seemed a little "off."

I was well aware that I'd told my story many times, but I felt a need to tell it one more time. After all, I'd nearly lost my life. Surely that was a more important subject of conversation than the tourist couple who stripped and walked naked down King Street to protest what they called price-gouging.

"Well, it seemed like forever to me," I said. "Days, literally. The crazy bitch came back several times to rant and rail about how y'all weren't responding to her ransom demands. Once she even waved a scissors in my face. Threatened to poke my eyes out. Now *that's* gouging."

Mama, seated across from us, shuddered. "Please, Abby, can't we talk about something else?"

"We could talk about my leg," C.J. said. The big gal had her leg propped up on an authentic Turkish ottoman, one that dated back to the earliest days of the Ottoman Empire. The leg was encased in a cast that sported more graffiti than the entire New York subway system.

I sighed. C.J. had a story to tell as well; one that had also been told a million times. But as long as she didn't make any detours to Shelby, I was willing to share the limelight with a friend.

"Tell us about your leg, dear," I said.

C.J. took a deep breath. "Well, when Dmitri came back to your house with the ring tied to his collar, I had just gotten off work. Greg wasn't home yet and Mozella was off gallivanting—"

"I was at church," Mama said, twirling her pearls in agitation. "I had a committee meeting."

"Anyway, I knew something had to be wrong. At first I thought of calling the police—"

"Which you should have done," Greg said.

C.J. squirmed. "But I couldn't be *sure* something was wrong. Abby does funny things like that, you know. Now where was I?"

"Calling the kettle black?" I suggested.

"The cat and the ring," Bob boomed. He and Rob had some kind of party to attend later in the evening, and I could tell they were beginning to get anxious for us to leave. They hadn't even bothered to drag out the expensive liqueurs.

C.J. nodded. "Yes, Dmitri. Well, I took him back outdoors and put him down. Abby, I told him that if you were in any trouble, he should lead me to you. But all he wanted to do was rub against my legs and purr. Finally, I had to bribe him with the promise of all the catnip he wanted.

"That seemed to work, but he sure as shooting didn't lead me on a straight course. I think we meandered through every backyard in Charleston. Honestly, Abby, you should teach that cat—"

"Please," I begged, "just finish the story."

"Well, we finally ended up in that crazy Mrs. Riffle's backyard. Suddenly Dmitri bounded up an oak tree like the catnip I'd promised him was somewhere at the top. I tried to follow as far as I could, but he disappeared into a dormer the size of a gnat's navel. It was when I tried to get back down that I fell and broke my leg."

Mama stood. "And then our intrepid heroine crawled to a neighbor's house and summoned help. Well, this has been a delightful evening, but I really must go. I hope y'all will excuse me."

Then everyone stood except for Greg and me. Something was rotten in Denmark, and it wasn't just Twice-Baked Eel.

"But," I protested, "C.J. hasn't even gotten to the part where the mayor called to congratulate her. Or how the police found all the tiles safe and sound in one of the other attic rooms, along with a bunch of other valuable stuff."

"Mayor shmayor," Mama said. "We can't keep the boys up all night."

"Where is it you must go, Mama?"

Mama's pearls became a blur of white. "Abby, some things are best left alone."

"Out with it, Mama!"

She hung her head, like a relay runner who'd dropped the torch in the last seconds of the race. "Gloria Krantz has invited us to a party."

"*Who?*"

C.J. picked up the torch. "You know, Abby. She's my neighbor. The one you call Gladys."

I looked from face to guilty face. "You were all invited?"

Greg gave my shoulder another bone-crushing squeeze. "Not me, hon."

"But she didn't invite *me*?"

"Abby, you don't even like her."

"That's not the point," I wailed. "All my friends are invited, even my very own mama, and—"

"Abby," Rob said gently, "we could stay home if that will make you feel better."

I considered that for a brief, selfish moment. Besides a fleeting feeling of power, I had nothing to gain

by such childishness. The repercussions were bound
to be endless, given that Mama has the memory of an
elephant on ginseng. But more importantly, it had just
occurred to me why Bob's eel seemed a little off; it
was the fishiest smelling thing in the room. For the
first time in months, my sweet baboo didn't smell like
a stranded tuna at low tide.

Rob read my mind and tossed me his keys. "You
two lock up."

"There are fresh sheets on the bed in the guest
room," Bob brayed.

"Ooh, ooh," C.J. hooted.

"TMI!" Mama cried, although she has no idea
what those initials stand for.

It's none of your business, but we went home first.
Then we locked Mama and C.J. out. Gloria Krantz's
party was no match for ours.